HOT AND FILTHY

THE DARK AND DAMAGED HEARTS SERIES,
BOOK 4.5

WHITLEY COX

ISBN: 978-1-7750910-7-3

DISCLAIMER

Please do not try any new sexual practices (BDSM or otherwise) without the guidance of an experienced practitioner. The author will not be held responsible for any loss, harm, injury or death resulting from use of the information contained in this book.

Make sure your e-reader files are stored and locked properly so no one under the age of eighteen can access them.

And on that note, I'd like to thank you for purchasing this book, and I hope you enjoy it. I certainly enjoyed writing it.

Thank you.
Whitley Cox

This one is for the husband again.
Life is bliss with you by my side.
I love you, and I can't wait until our next dive!
xoxo

Just a bit about this book...

I never intended to write a third James and Emma book, but these two are a part of me. They were the first characters I ever created, and I just haven't been able to let them go. Their romance was so tumultuous and raw, their love story so full of angst and darkness, that I wanted to write something for them that was full of happiness, full of light and full of promise. Yes, *Sex, Heat and Hunger* had a happily ever after, but I believe James and Emma deserve more than that; my readers deserve more.

This is the story of their honeymoon. Please take note, unlike the title of the series, *The Dark and Damaged Hearts,* there is no darkness in this book. It's full of love, fun and a whole lot of sex, with some scuba diving thrown in for good measure.

This book can be read as a stand-alone, but in order to truly understand the characters, their struggles, personalities and the journey of their love, it is recommended that you read it after *Sex, Heat and Hunger: Parts 1 and 2.*

PROLOGUE

JAMES

"Are you nervous?" Justin asked as we stood milling around the back yard. Guests were slowly filing in and taking their seats in the white folding chairs on either side of the aisle.

I shook my head and tossed my sunglasses on. The sun was high and mighty, and I could already see a couple of bald heads turning a frightening shade of pink.

"Not in the least. Were you?"

He snorted. "Nervous? Naw. Giddy, excited, impatient, yeah. But nervous, not at all."

I nodded. "That's how I feel."

He slapped me on the back. "You could have fooled me, dude. You're grinding your teeth like a rabid badger and teetering back and forth on your feet like a guy getting ready to see his first real boob."

I shot him an irritated look, but he just started laughing. I was about to say something snide, only we were interrupted by a frenzy of frilly dresses and flying pigtails as two adorable whirling dervishes came running full tilt at his shins.

"Daddy!" Chloe squealed as she lunged into his arms, whether he was ready for her or not.

Justin knelt down and let out an exaggerated *oof* when she slammed into his chest. He scooped up the two-year-old and plopped her on his hip, while Maggie, the five-year-old, came up quietly behind her sister and leaned into her father's leg. He ran his hand affectionately down the back of her head.

"Shouldn't you two be getting ready do your flower girl thing?" he asked, planting a big smacking smooch on Chloe's chubby cheek.

"Auntie Emma is running late," Maggie said matter-of-factly.

Justin's eyes found mine, and a flash of concern zoomed through his aqua orbs, but he dismissed it as fast as he could.

"Running late how, sweetie?" he asked.

Maggie's eyes flew up to mine, and she bit her lip for a second. "Something about a dress needing to be hemmed."

I felt my shoulders relax. *Had I been worried that she'd bailed? Shit!*

"Ah!" Justin said with a big nod. "Makes sense. Everything has to be perfect today, including dress hems."

Maggie nodded absentmindedly. Her eyes fixated instead on Emma's brother Lewis, who was sitting next to her other brother, Peter, and his partner, Noah. Peter had come out of the closet early last year, to the surprise the entire family, and revealed that he'd been in a loving relationship with Noah for eighteen months. The two were very happy and had already moved in together and purchased two French Bulldogs, names Dolly and Cher.

I recognized the look in Maggie's eyes. Intense. Unwavering. Burning. It was a look I knew well. It was the same look I gave my future wife every minute of every day. Maggie was in love with Lewis. Poor kid. Unrequited love can be tough, especially when all that's really keeping you apart is a twenty-year age gap and the fact that he lives in a different city and doesn't even know you exist. I tried to hide my snort and instead said a small thank-you to the universe that a twelve-year age gap hadn't deterred my bride and I from taking the leap. Everything inside me thrummed to life when I thought of Emma; the world became vibrant and clear. And when she was near, and I got to touch her, all I could think of and crave was her body beneath mine, and raw, primal *sex*. The woman was my world.

But she also drove me crazy. So headstrong and feisty. My sister has always said I needed a strong woman, one who was independent and fierce; demanding and stubborn, and hell if I hadn't found her and then some. Sitting alone in a bar, stood up by her best friend who'd come down with food poisoning.

Nobody knew this, not even my bride, but I'd eventually found out which sushi restaurant had given Alyssa food poisoning. And instead of turning the restaurant into the health inspector (they were violating a few health codes when I'd walked in) I paid for a topnotch team to come in a re-vamp the whole restaurant, re-train the staff and overhaul their menu (you know, like Gordon Ramsay does with *Kitchen Nightmares*). Then I'd sent the owners, who were overworked and worn thin, on a cruise. If it hadn't been for their bad fish, I may have never met the woman who had made me whole again, so I wanted to thank them.

But my future wife and I butted heads often enough, especially during those first few months. But we always seem to meet in the middle in the end. It's the kind of friction that works for us. Compromises and apologies. Talking it out. Before Emma I hadn't been a big talker. And certainly not about my feelings or my past. But she made me want to open up. I demanded complete honesty from her, no lies, no secrets, and in turn I gave her the same. There was nothing but trust between us now. Because Emma was made for me. Perfection in a feisty, curvy, bossy little blonde package with the biggest heart and sexiest laugh, and no matter what, I could never get enough of her, and I knew I never would.

The marriage commissioner came out of the house and nodded at me. "Looks like we're just about ready, Mr. Shaw."

I nodded back, an immediate rush of adrenaline careening through my body, as if I had just stepped off the world's most extreme roller coaster.

"Ready, bud?" Justin laughed, taking in my suddenly frazzled demeanor. The man was my best friend, had been for the past twenty years. He knew me better than anyone — well, maybe not Emma — but he knew me well enough to tell that I was, in fact, a tad nervous.

Justin put Chloe down, her older sister grabbed her hand, and the two ran off toward the house giggling, pigtails flying again.

"Okay," Justin said, as the two of us made our way up the aisle toward the wisteria-adorned arch I'd built earlier in the year for this very day. Emma had planted the flowers with the hopes that they'd climb the lattice in time for the wedding. "It's me ... let's talk for a second. What's wrong?"

I swallowed past the lump in my throat and stood on the right side of where the marriage commissioner would soon stand. She was just double-checking the table where we'd sign everything to make it official.

"What if I'm a shit husband?" I finally asked, not looking at him. I couldn't look at him. I couldn't take my eyes from the door.

I didn't have to see him to know he was rolling his eyes. "You probably will be from time to time. You can be an asshole. But Emma's a ballbuster, and she won't take your shit. Has she taken your shit yet?"

"No."

"So what makes you think she's going to start accepting it now?"

I swallowed again. "I don't know."

"She loves you, man. Like walk across hot coals or Lego for you, loves you. And you're a better man because of her. You were a miserable fuck before."

"I know."

"Just don't be an asshole. Calm the jealousy, calm the temper and keep the lines of communication open. If there's anything I've learned from watching my parents' marriage fail, and then when Kendra and I nearly ended, it's that *not* talking *doesn't* work. Secrets are relationship kryptonite. And you of all people, *Superman*, should know to steer clear of kryptonite ... at least the green kind."

I shook my head while giving him a slanted look. Leave it to Justin to toss in a superhero reference. His comic-book geek was out in full force this afternoon.

He just grinned and slapped my back again. "Ah, don't overthink it. Marriage is easy. Talk, fuck and fuck some more. And then once you're done fucking, talk some more. And then talk about how much fun it is to fuck and how you can't wait to fuck again. Toss in some respect, appreciation and a couple compliments a day and you're golden. All these people who say that the sex ends when you get married are obviously marrying the wrong people. It doesn't end, it just gets better. But then introduce kids into the mix and well ... you just learn how to be quick, sneaky and quiet about it. And sometimes, yes, after a night of barfing toddlers and colicky newborns, sleep is more appealing than a quick bone. But the sex certainly doesn't end when you tie the knot. Not in a *good* marriage anyway."

"It's really that easy, eh?"

"Yup."

The pigtailed pixies poked their heads out the door, and the music changed. I straightened up and clasped my hands in front of me, eyes fixed on the door where Maggie and Chloe stood like small fairy princesses with their matching purple dresses and flower crowns.

They started to walk down the aisle, tossing petals haphazardly onto the grass, a handful here and then one petal there. It was adorable, and the small crowd of guests thought the same. One day *very* soon I hoped to have my own kids to look at adoringly. And with any luck, they'd be arriving roughly nine months from now. Oohs and aws and snaps of the photographer's camera overlapped the soft din of the unobtrusive violin music. The girls approached the front of the aisle and shot their father big matching grins before Kendra, their mother, held out her hands and ushered them off to the side with her.

Next was Alyssa, Emma's best friend and matron of honor, in a simple lilac (or so my fiancée had educated me) dress that swept the floor. I liked the woman, but fuck, she walked slowly. *Hurry the hell up; you're not who I want to see. You're not who I* need *to see.*

She had a cocky smirk on her face as she passed me, taking up her post on the other side of the marriage commissioner. And then she winked. The woman was a ballbuster, too.

I swallowed. I wasn't sure I'd blinked since the flower girls came down the aisle. *Where is Emma? Where is my bride? Where is my wife?*

And then the music changed, everyone stood up, and there she was, standing next to her parents in the doorway of our home, the sun shining down on her like the lifesaving angel that she was. Her long flaxen hair glowed around her shoulders, while her dress made my heart race, my palms sweaty and my cock twitch inside my pants.

Her eyes found mine, and she smiled, the same smile that nearly three years ago had changed my whole life, my whole world, flipped it on its head and made me want more than just an easy lay and success. A smile that made me want a family, a future and someone to share it all with. God, would the day ever come when I would see her and not feel the earth quake and rumble beneath my feet? I certainly hoped not.

CHAPTER 1

EMMA

"Are you nervous?" Alyssa asked as she placed the flower crown on top of my head. We were standing upstairs in the master bedroom, my mother and grandmother flitting around behind us, frantically trying to sew the frayed hem of my Aunt Eleanor's dress.

I grinned at Alyssa in the mirror and bit my lip as I adjusted the flowers. "Not in the slightest. Giddy is more like it."

Her eyes twinkled. "I'm not sure I've ever met a man more head-over-heels in love with someone than your groom. The man would walk over glass ... hell, he'd walk over Lego for you."

I smiled again, my cheeks burning from how mushy thoughts of my future husband made me. "I'd walk over Lego for him, too."

"Everyone ready?" my mother asked, a rosy flush to her own high cheekbones as she stood up from the floor, the sewing needle and thread still between her lips. She was a beautiful woman, Anita Everly. With peaches and cream skin and a long slender neck, which she showed off with her short blonde pixie cut, she was the definition of a classic beauty.

I let out a big sigh and locked eyes with my mother in the mirror. We had the same hazel eyes, though hers held the kind of wisdom and compassion I only hoped to have one day. She gave me a teary-eyed smile.

"You bet!" I smiled back, emotion and the sudden realization of what I was about to go and do hitting me in the solar plexus like a swift kick. "Let's go and get me hitched!"

"There's my baby girl," my dad said, meeting my mother and I at the foot of the stairs, his own eyes starting to show signs of needing a tissue.

He looped his arm through mine, and my mother took up sentry on the other side, while I clutched the bouquet I'd made from my own garden flowers in my sweaty fist.

"You look beautiful, honey."

"Thanks, Dad."

He glanced down at my feet, where my red painted toes just peeked out from beneath my flowy Grecian-style gown. "Still going with the no shoe thing, eh?"

I rolled my eyes. "It's a backyard wedding. The grass is soft, and although we all know I love me some heels, I'd rather not trip on my wedding day. Besides, it goes with the whole Boho fairy princess thing I'm doing."

I awkwardly gestured to my off-white halter dress and flower crown on top of my beachy, wavy hair. He just snorted a laugh and rolled his green eyes, smiling at me like only a father getting ready to give his only daughter away could, with heavily reined-in emotion and glowing pride.

I'm not a pomp and circumstance kind of girl, and James is certainly not a pomp and circumstance kind of guy. He's not flashy, and neither of us was into the big church wedding with hundreds of people we hardly knew. We wanted simple, tasteful and, most of all, relaxing. James isn't into big crowds, and he hates being the center of attention, so I took great care to make the day as minimally stressful and with the least amount of attention focused on him as possible, while still being fun for our guests. And what better way than a DIY, backyard BBQ wedding with just close friends and family? So, bare feet and a flower crown just seemed to fit the vibe we were jonesing for.

"Nervous?" my dad asked.

I swallowed. "Not at all. You?"

His jaw shook slightly, but he didn't say anything; his expression was tangible.

Two tiny garden fairies in matching purple dresses and crowns of baby's breath bounded down the aisle, sprinkling flower petals as they went. They might not be blood, but they were my nieces in every other way that mattered, and I was so happy they were sharing in our special day. Alyssa was next out the French doors, stopping at the edge of the patio and tossing her shoulders back. She glanced behind her and gave me a big wink and a smile before stepping down onto the soft grass toward the altar.

"I think you might have found someone who loves you more than we do," my mum said as we made our way through the living room toward the open doors, the music in the back yard drawing us like the Pied Piper.

"As it should be," my father said stoically.

He pulled me tighter against him and then turned his head and pecked me on the temple. He had to bend down a wee bit, though, as my dad is a tall drink of water and my head barely brushes his shoulders.

"We love you, baby girl," he choked, taking a deep breath.

I squeezed both their arms and gave them each one final look before the daylight of the back yard dazzled my eyes.

"I love you guys, too."

And then the big tall evergreens shielded the sun, and my groom finally came into view, standing handsome and regal next to his best friend, while his cobalt eyes twinkled and his mouth, that devilish, talented, delicious mouth of his, curled up into the most jaw-dropping —and panty-dropping—smile I'd ever seen.

"Well, *Mrs. Shaw* ... God, I'm never going to grow tired of calling you that, you know that, right?" James growled, pulling me onto his lap in the back of the limo.

He nuzzled my neck while his hand made its way up my shirt, and he started pulling on the cup of my bra. I squeaked and squirmed when he tweaked the hard and achy bud, loving the bite of pain and the zing of need it sent to my core.

"Shall we consummate the marriage here and now? Or can you wait until we board the jet?"

I chuckled low and let my hand drift to the front of his shorts, unzipping him and worming my fingers in until I felt the hard column of flesh I just couldn't get enough of.

"It's not *that* long of a drive to the airport," I purred. "And I certainly hope the consummation will take more than five minutes. So ..." I dropped to my knees. "Let's just do this until we get to the jet, where there is a big, beautiful bed, and you can fuck your new wife properly." And then I pulled down his shorts, dipped my head low and took him into my mouth.

His fingers found their way into my hair, and he pulled on my scalp, setting the pace he wanted, hard and fast, just like our love. I'd loved this man almost instantly, craved him from our first kiss. He was my addiction, and I hungered for him constantly. There was no rehab or detox program in the world that could kick me of my James habit, not that I wanted one. The man was my everything, and now, finally, after almost two and a half years together, he was my husband. We'd been through hell and back both on our own and together. Fought past demons and weathered storms no couple or person should ever have to face. He'd torn down his walls for me. Let me inside, revealed his true self and the heavy weight and guilt he carried around on those impossibly broad shoulders of his. But now that guilt, those problems weren't just his. We were in this together and even though I knew James would never truly forgive himself or let go entirely of his haunting past, at least now I could help carry the weight. Relieve him of the burden just a bit, and be there to rub out the knots and tired muscles at the end of the day.

"God, Emma ... that fucking mouth ..." he groaned, bucking his hips up off the leather of the seat. "Yes, you filthy girl. Suck it hard."

I couldn't help but smile as I took him to the back of my throat, my fist rhythmically pumping him root to tip; I loved the effect I had on him, loved how easily I could bring him to his knees while I pleasured him on mine. He was a bossy fucker, incapable of submitting, but when he was in my mouth, he was completely at my mercy. I could ask him for anything, and he'd never say "no." Not that I asked for much, and not that he'd ever denied me. But when I was on my knees, the man was under my spell, and I was in control as much as he liked to think he was.

I flattened out my tongue and grazed the entire surface area up his shaft, feeling the thick roping veins and the silky, soft crown. He was perfect. Designed by the gods. Tall and muscular with a strong, chiseled jaw and dark, luscious, wavy hair that tumbled just over his forehead and ears. Not too long and unruly, but just roguish enough. I loved nothing more than burying my fingers in it, and pulling on the ends, especially when his head was bobbing up and down between my legs.

I snaked my other hand beneath him and cupped his balls, gently pulling and rolling them in my palm until I earned that extra moan I coveted, the moan that told me he loved it and he wanted more. The moan that told me he was getting close, barely holding on, pacing that narrow edge and about to tip over.

His cadence picked up, and he started to jerk on my head, really forcing me down hard onto his cock, until it knocked my tonsils and I fought to suppress my gag reflex. And fuck if I didn't love it. I loved that I could drive him wild.

I sucked hard on the crown when I brought him back to my lips, flicking the tip, the small hole at the top with my tongue, wedging it in just enough to earn another moan, before I plunged him back to my throat again. In and out I fucked him with my mouth until his rhythm started to falter and I knew he was close.

I swallowed when he bottomed out in my throat again, knowing that the contraction of my muscles might just kick him over the cliff. I pulled down slightly on his balls with my one hand, and down on his shaft with the other, hummed slightly and deep throated as much as I could, swallowing again. And damn if that didn't do the trick.

He snarled above me as his fingers loosened their death grip in my hair, his cock pulsing inside my mouth, filling me with his warm, salty semen. I swallowed again, letting it flow across my tongue and down my throat, reveling in his canticle of pleasure.

I licked him clean and then gently tucked him back into his shorts, taking great care not to snag him in his zipper. Then big, strong hands came up under my arms, and I was hauled off the floor and thrown onto my back on the cool leather. Growling low and deep in his throat, he pinned me beneath him, his mouth capturing mine.

He groaned against my lips as his fingers found a nipple again. "Oh, *Mrs. Shaw.* I'm not sure I can wait until the plane to fuck you."

CHAPTER 2

We boarded Justin's jet a short while later, James having managed to get me off with his mouth in the back of the limo—twice—before we pulled up to the Departures gate and were forced to make ourselves semi-presentable for the public again. But it was late at night and hardly anyone was around, so the fact that my T-shirt was on inside-out and my hair was a proverbial train wreck seemed to go unnoticed by the two women who loaded our luggage, and if they did notice, they didn't say anything.

They were both too mesmerized by my gorgeous husband, his sapphire eyes and his casually messy hair that stuck out in every direction in chunky black waves, because I'd been pulling on it for dear life just a short while ago as he ate me out with reckless abandon. And why wouldn't they ogle him? Eye-fuck the bejesus out of him. He was perfection. Potent. Vigorous. Strong. Dangerous and untameable. An alpha in the prime of his life. Wildly successful and unbelievably attractive. The perfect specimen to mate with. And he was all mine, forever and always.

"All right, Mr. and Mrs. Shaw," the pilot said with a smile as we sat in the plush cream leather seats of Justin's private jet. "Next stop, Papeete, French Polynesia. You two just sit back and relax and let the honeymoon start now. Mr. Williams has instructed me not to bother you with anything, so if you need something, just call the cockpit, all right?"

James leaned forward in his seat but didn't remove his arm from around my shoulder, making the pilot step forward. He extended his hand toward the handlebar-mustached man and thanked him.

"Thank you," I said shyly, itching to get in the air and beneath my new husband. It was a long flight to Tahiti, and I planned to spend the majority of it enjoying the rock solid body of my man. Sleep was for suckers. I'd sleep when I was dead.

The captain nodded and offered me a small smile before joining his co-pilot in the cockpit and shutting the door, leaving me alone with my husband, the air around us crackling and sizzling with the desperate need to get to the back of the plane and into the enormous bed.

This wasn't the first time we'd been on Justin's private jet, or the first time we'd joined the mile-high club, but this was the first time we'd be doing it as husband and wife, and somehow it felt different. There was this unexpected frisson of nerves that wandered up and down my spine while butterflies careened and bumped into one another in my belly.

James pulled me tighter against him and kissed my temple. "You tired?"

"No. You?"

"No."

"So, uh ..."

His chuckle was deep and menacing and made my lady parts tingle. "Eager, are we?"

"Aren't you?" I asked, looking up into eyes. The jet lurched, and we started to taxi down the runway.

He grabbed my hand and brought it down to the front of his shorts. "What do you think?"

I swallowed. We'd made love hundreds if not thousands of times, but it never grew old, it never grew boring, and each and every time I knew he was hard I ached to have him inside me. The man was a drug. I gently cupped him, and he pushed his pelvis up into my hand.

"Do we, uh ... do we *have* to wait until we're airborne?" I asked, licking my lips. I'd only just had him in my mouth, and already I wanted more.

His grin was wily as he reached across my lap and undid my seat-belt. His hands deliberately took their sweet time, while his arm brushed my breasts and his breath was warm on my neck. Our eyes locked for just a brief moment before he slid out of his seat onto the floor, dragging my shorts with him.

He spread my lips with his fingers and blew cool air onto my already wet and swollen core while a curious finger gently traced my folds and dipped inside.

"You're so wet," he purred, denying me what I sorely needed and instead nipping my inner thigh.

I pushed up with my hips. "For you, always."

His tongue darted out, and he flicked the top of my clit. I nearly fell off the seat. A triumphant chuckle rumbled low in his chest as he planted a light kiss on my mound, his fingers continuing with their inquisitive quest, plunging in and out of me, grazing my walls and hitting that sweet spot inside.

"James," I said breathlessly. "No more playing ... please."

His eyes darted up to mine, while his tongue shot out again and swept up my cleft. And then his lips enclosed my clit and he sucked.

"James!" I pleaded.

He lifted his head from my lap. "Yes, *Mrs. Shaw*?"

"Fuck your wife, for Christ's sake!"

Like a stealthy ninja, he leapt up from his spot on the floor and scooped me up. "Bossy little horndog I married." He laughed, his smile salacious and full of mischief. Eating up the distance to the bedroom in just a few big strides, he opened the door, and we were greeted with a big, beautiful queen-size bed and Egyptian cotton.

He tossed me onto the mattress with enough force to make me bounce, and then he stood there at the foot of it, staring at me.

I blinked at him. What the hell was he waiting for? *Ravish me! Fuck me! Fuck your wife!*

"W-what's wrong?" I asked, angling up onto my elbows and giving him a wary look. I couldn't get a read on him. The man was a master at hiding his emotions, donning that unreadable mask of indifference, so that you had no idea what he was thinking or how he was feeling.

He shook his head slightly. "Nothing's wrong. I ... I just can't believe you're my wife." He swallowed but didn't move. I wasn't even sure he was blinking.

I smiled. He wasn't a big one for sharing his feelings, but he did for me. I knew it made him uncomfortable, knew it was a big challenge and something he hated doing, showing his vulnerable side, but he did it for me. He tore his walls down for me.

I reached for him. "For the rest of our lives."

His Adam's apple bobbed heavy and thick in his long, sexy throat. "I love you so much, Emma. I don't want to fuck this up. I can't lose you ... not ever."

I flipped over onto my stomach and then up onto all fours, prowling forward, standing up on my knees in front of him at the edge of the bed. We were nearly eye-to-eye, a rare occasion, as he's nearly as tall as my dad and stands a good foot taller than me. I draped my arms around his neck and pressed my chest against him, heart to heart, eye to eye, so that all we saw, all we felt, was each other.

"I love you, too. And you won't lose me. We're forever, you and I. This is the real deal."

A muscle along the edge of his jaw ticked with pent-up emotion. How could I let him know that his worries were for naught? That we were eternal, that my love for him was so deep and unwavering that his fears were unfounded and he couldn't, wouldn't lose me, even if he tried?

"I was such a miserable fucker before you met me, Emma." He blinked, finally. His eyes were so full of roiling emotions, my heart ached at the need to reassure him and quell his worries.

"I know," I said quietly. "But you're not now."

"Because of you."

"Because you wanted to change. Because you wanted to be happy."

"*You* make me happy."

"James, where is all this coming from? You're kind of freaking me out. This is our honeymoon. I married you today. If I wasn't all in from here to the end of time, I wouldn't have said 'I do.'"

"I know," he sighed, his hands finally finding their way to my hips.

"A second ago, you were getting ready to fuck me senseless. What's changed?"

He paused for a second, and I lifted one eyebrow quizzically.

"When we consummate our marriage, that's it. No annulment. It'd be divorce, and it's just hitting me in a weird way. I don't want to divorce you."

"But you want to get an annulment?" Now he was really starting to scare me.

He shook his head. "No, not ever. It's just ... that's it, that seals the deal. The ceremony, the paperwork, that's all a formality. This, you and I, together like this, this is us, the real us. And our first time as husband and wife, it's ..."

"Special."

He nodded. "Yeah. Special. Remember when you put all this expectation on our first time together, to the point where you decided that there was too much pressure and just knocked on my door and told me to fuck you right then and there, rather than waiting for after our date?"

I snorted and nodded. It was a hard thing to forget. I'd been so nervous about going to bed with James for the first time. He was so experienced, so much older, and he'd been with over a hundred women, whereas I'd only been with three men before him, and one of those had been a sexually oppressive and abusive relationship. I had been terrified I wouldn't be able to hold a candle to any of the other women he'd slept with and that he'd find me boring and vanilla and not worth his time.

So the afternoon before our date, I'd driven to his house and surprised him, saying that we needed to have sex then and there. So that by the time the evening rolled around there would be no more nerves, we'd know what we were getting ourselves into, and that initial first-time awkwardness wouldn't be hanging over us like an ominous fog.

"So, you put all this pressure on yourself for our first time as husband and wife, and now you're nervous?" I asked, still trying to understand where his head was.

He lifted one shoulder cavalierly. "I guess."

I unlaced my fingers from behind his neck, where I'd been mindlessly playing with the hair at the nape, dragging them down his granite-hard torso and to the hem of his shirt. I drew it up over his head and tossed it to the floor. His shorts were next, followed by his black boxer briefs, until he stood in front of me, naked and hard and perfect.

I started to kiss up and down his neck, his pulse beating fast and true beneath my lips, while I let my hand drift down his abdomen, past the light dusting of hair, until his cock lay hard and thick in my palm. I stroked him as I peppered hot, wet kisses along his jaw and neck and chest, his body slowly relaxing with each kiss.

"There is nothing to be nervous about," I said softly, giving a slight tug to his shaft and earning a quick inhale from him. "I love you, James. You are mine forever. And I'm never letting you go. No annulment, no divorce, nothing ever. We're going to grow old and gray and wrinkly together."

He huffed a forced laugh.

I pulled harder on his cock. "I mean it. Stop thinking these thoughts. Stop worrying, stop fretting, lose the nerves, and make love to your wife."

His eyes flashed hot molten fire, and I watched as something finally clicked in that gorgeous brain of his.

"You're a bossy little horndog," he said again, a glimmer of humor back in his eyes, along with a look that said, "I'm ready to fuck you until your brain is mush."

Yes! Finally!

"I'm *your* bossy little horndog," I said sassily. "And I'm growing rather impatient. We're at 30,000 feet, and you're still not inside me. What the hell, Shaw?" Seriously, dude, enough with the freakin' chit-chat and fuck your damn wife!

"Impatient?" he challenged, the nerves from earlier gone and my confident and dominant man back. "Well, that little bit of attitude has earned your ass a couple of hard smacks, *wife* of mine. You'll wait as long as I want you to, you got that? Perhaps I'll tie you to the bedposts too. Go have a shower. Come out dripping wet and then tan your ass some more. What do you think of that?"

Hells yes! Please, oh please!

I grinned wickedly and then pulled my T-shirt over my head and quickly unhooked my bra. "Would you like to spank me now ... *husband*?" I asked.

The thought passed across his face for a brief second, but then he shook his head. "No. Right now I'm going to fuck my new wife properly, and then maybe later I'll punish her for that bit of sass. Punish her properly. You have no idea the kinky shit I've packed for this trip, princess. By the end of this honeymoon, you're going to have bruises and bite marks, a tender ass and chafed wrists from my shackles." He lunged forward, and I was once again pinned beneath him. I squealed as he tackled me.

Kinky shit, hooray!

I sighed when I felt his weight on me. "Yes," I said breathlessly, arching my hips up to meet his grinding pelvis, eager to take all of him.

He lifted both my hands up and over my head and held them there with one of his, restraining me so that there wasn't anything I could do besides bend to his will. I submitted entirely and let his body take mine where it wanted to go, where it needed to go. He ground against me again, and I spread my legs wider, desperate for him. His gaze found mine, and without a word, he lifted up and then slammed home, sheathing himself to the hilt in one solid thrust.

"Oh, God!" I cried, finally feeling full. "Yes!"

"So good!" he grunted, hammering into me with feral intent, the primitive urge to fuck coming out as he claimed my body as his in every way that mattered. "Mine!"

"Yours!" I agreed, lifting my hips up to meet him thrust for thrust, wrapping my legs around his trunk, the heel of my foot wedging its way between his clenching butt cheeks.

His teeth grazed my collarbone and I inhaled quickly. I loved the pain. I loved everything he did to me, every bite, every scratch, every spank. There wasn't anything James did to my body that I didn't want more of.

"Mine!" he roared again, nipping my chin and then finally finding my lips. I reared up and shoved my tongue into his mouth, challenging his to a duel, urging him to fuck me just as roughly with his tongue as his cock was fucking my pussy.

In and out, in and out he plunged, the sweat on our skin causing our bodies to glide against each other, the room filling with nothing but the savage grunts and moans of our passion. This was what I'd wanted. This was what I'd needed. This was who he was when we were together, the true James, the real, raw and hungry man I fell in love with. Who possessed me, mind, body and soul. Whom I'd pledged my life to, for better or for worse, for the rest of our days. This was the crazy fucker, the incredible fucker, I'd married.

I loved every part of him, including the sentimental part, but I knew that it wasn't an easy part of him to expose. He kept those feelings buried deep and rarely brought them out, so even after all this time, it was still startling to hear such heartrending words from him, to hear his fears and his feelings. And although I knew he wasn't lying to me, I also knew it wasn't easy.

What came easy to James was fucking. The real James liked to fuck rough and he liked to fuck hard. Making a woman come until she passed out was a hobby and one he took very seriously. So for him to be nervous to consummate our marriage left me puzzled. Because the real James was ruthless, calculating and confident, with a menacing demeanor that frightened most people when they first met him, only for his dazzling smile and generous nature to eventually win them over.

But behind that enigmatic smile were years of pain, years of heartache and years of guilt. He'd lost his twin brother to leukemia when the boys were thirteen, and James blamed himself because he wasn't a donor match. Andy's death had sent the entire family into a fiery tailspin of doom and despair, with James becoming angry and depressed. His parents separated for a time; his father tried to commit suicide, and his mother checked out and hired a nanny. His sister Amy rebelled, becoming this partying wild child that hardly anyone could control, aside from maybe her baseball coach. Throw in some maniacal ex-girlfriends over the years, an endless stream of emotionless fucks with random women, and when I met him, he was scarcely a shell of a man, living to work, not working to live. But now, now he was different. He loved life, he loved me and he finally, I think, loved himself.

He continued to drill me, pounding harder and harder, his bucking relentless and growing more and more fierce as the minutes ticked by. I was a maelstrom of divine sensations. His pelvic bone hit my clit just right, while the way his cock split me open and rubbed against that tender, luscious spot inside had my eyes rolling into the back of my head and my body arching against his, desperate for more. He still had my hands pinned above my head, and his free hand was braced beside me, his bicep rippling with the strain of carrying his weight. But he was meticulous in his devotion and knew I needed more. He dipped his head low and latched onto a nipple, pulling and then flicking it with his tongue, reveling in my moan and then doing it again.

"God, I love fucking you," he purred, letting his tongue trace my chest, only to take the other hard peak into his mouth and deliver the same delicious torment. Gentle tugs of suction until the tender point ached and my pussy clenched on instinct. "So fucking beautiful."

I groaned again as he drew the tight bud between his teeth. "Oh God, James, I'm so close."

"Fuck, baby, you're going to come so hard for me. You're going to come hard for me all night, right?"

All I could do was nod and whimper. My body was ready to detonate; I couldn't think straight. Fuck, what the hell was my name? Where were we?

"I'm going to come!" I whined, my whole body winding up into a fever pitch as he thundered into me harder and faster than ever before.

"Come, my sexy fucking wife!" he panted. "Come hard." And then he released my hands from his fist, braced himself above me and started to just go to town, harder and harder, until I thought he was going to shatter my pelvis with his, or at the very least split me in half. But fuck, it felt good. It felt good inside, and it felt good to watch him finally let go of his worries and fears and embrace his true beast and claim me.

I clawed at his back and pulled him against me. "James!" I cried as my body bowed on the bed and I let go, the orgasm unfurling in my belly and spreading out through each limb, to the tips of my hair and my crimson-painted toes.

I shut my eyes and let it take over. Bright lights and flashes of color burst like fireworks behind my lids, while a faint buzzing sound filled my ears, followed by the pounding of my own pulse. Was that angels singing in the background, too? I couldn't tell. I convulsed beneath him, literally shook and jostled as if I were having a seizure. My body no longer belonged to me; it belonged to the pleasure, and it would do with me as it pleased.

Clenching my muscles around him, I encouraged him to join me on the fall. His gaze found mine. His eyes were near black, dilated and filled with lust, while his nostrils flared like those of a predator who'd just caught the scent of his prey ... or his mate.

"Come with me," I whispered, my own orgasm not yet done and making my words come out in a garbled mess.

He bared his teeth, gave me one good and powerful final thrust and then came undone. His head fell to the crook of my neck and his teeth pierced my shoulder, while a slew of snarls and incoherent filth spewed from his lips. I rode out the rest of my release with him, milking him, squeezing him, loving him.

We lay there like that for a brief moment, let our heart rates return to rest and our brains find their correct synapses again. I still wasn't entirely sure what my name was.

"Well, that was some consummation there, *husband*," I giggled, finally finding my brain again and tracing my nails up and down his back, enjoying the feeling of his soft skin and hard muscles beneath my fingertips, the perfect definition of my man, hard and soft and fucking perfect.

He was quiet. I thought for sure he was going to give me a "mhmm" or a "you bet your sweet ass, princess," but he didn't say anything. I knew he was still alive; his cock was still nestled deep and hard inside me, and I could feel his warm breath on my neck. Had he fallen asleep?

"James?"

"Erm?"

"You okay?"

Finally, he propped himself up on one arm and leaned over to look at me. "I am. Are you? I didn't hurt you, did I?"

I smiled and cupped his cheek, bringing his mouth down to mine for a brief kiss.

"Not at all. I'm glad you're back. I was worried for a second that you'd disappeared on me."

His Adam's apple bobbed big and sexy in this throat. "You scare the fucking daylights out of me, Emma. I just don't want to screw this up."

"You're not, and you won't. Stop worrying and instead fuck me like that again. That's the man I fell in love with. That's the man I married. The warrior, the beast, the Dominant."

His chest bobbed in silent laughter. "Who are we kidding, woman? You have me by the fucking balls." And then he rolled off me and grabbed my hand. "Come on, let's go have a sexy shower."

CHAPTER 3

We landed in Papeete, on the island of Tahiti, roughly around lunchtime the following day. James had fucked me senseless for the majority of our flight, only allowing me a few hours of sleep, until he shoved his head between my legs and woke me up the way a good husband should.

We wasted no time, hopped in our rented jeep and hightailed it to the dock, where lo and behold, the most beautiful vessel awaited us.

"I can't believe this boat is just for us!" I gushed as I wandered around the top deck, my jaw nearly hitting the floor, while the sun shone overhead with glaring intensity. I'd forgotten to put on sunscreen, and already my shoulders were starting to tingle.

"You, me, the fishies and a couple of deckhands, princess. Sailing around French Polynesia for six whole weeks." James grinned, coming up behind me and wrapping his arms around my waist. His chin fell to the crook of my neck, and we started to sway.

"We could have gone with a smaller boat," I chided. "I mean, you have your own boat, so you're not ignorant when it comes to captaining a ship. And now we have to be careful about where we get jiggy with it because of Lola and Ezra."

"Naw," he scoffed. "They're cool. I told them to keep a low profile and that we won't require much of them. Just help with dive equipment and steering and mooring. I thought about renting a smaller one, and just the two of us sailing around, but all that time captaining and sailing, messing around with dive gear and having to cook would take time away from you, and me fucking you. So a big boat with a staff it is."

I rolled my eyes and let my neck loll to the side. His teeth grazed up my pulsing vein, and I pushed my butt into him. He was hard as a rock.

"Again?" I sighed, giving my hips a little wiggle. He pressed himself against me with a groan.

"If I could fuck you every minute of every day, I would."

"Hmmm," I hummed, looking out to sea and the horizon; we were in paradise and in James' arms I was in heaven. "I feel the same."

"Do you?" he asked, spinning me around so that we were face to face. "So if I tossed you on that deck chair over there and had my way with you for the rest of the afternoon, you wouldn't complain?" His eyes glimmered with mischief, while his mouth curled up into a crafty grin.

"Your butt cheeks might get a little burned," I teased.

He gripped me by the elbows and hauled me across the deck to the waiting lounge chair, tossing me down onto the fabric. I'd chosen to wear a skirt, so there was no stripping needed, and before I could blink, he was on his belly and pushing the hem of my skirt up my waist while moving my bathing-suit bottoms to the side.

"I love that you shave," he said, wasting no time and flicking out his tongue against my clit. My whole body shook. "Nothing between me and your sweet pink pussy, ever." And then he dove in, lips, tongue and fingers, the whole shebang. Swirling and twisting, plunging and plundering, until I was a mewling, sopping wet mess, and my cheeks were beginning to get warm and probably pink from the ruthless sun.

"I ... I don't know about all day there, stud," I said, already out of breath. "We might have to take things to the shade for a bit." I shamelessly pushed my hips up into his face, letting his nose graze my clit, while his tongue fucked me, hard and swift. A curious finger made its way further beneath me, and he pushed, demanding I give him refuge.

I arched my back to grant him access, and he slipped inside. I was so wet, so saturated with need that he had zero problems. We rarely used lube these days; we just didn't need it.

He hummed against my cleft, sending a jolt of pleasure careening through me.

"One quick orgasm for me, baby, and then I'll save you from the sun and go fuck you down below in our bed."

"You're relentless," I sighed, my hands weaving their way into his hair and gently pulling on his scalp.

"Obsessed is a better word." And then he closed his lips around my clit, pushed two fingers inside my pussy and started to scissor.

I was close, so damn close. Writhing on the deck chair, with burned cheeks and aching nipples, under the hot tropical sun, close.

"I can feel it, Emma. Let go, baby. You're right there," he hummed again, his buzzing lips sending another zing of need through my body.

I fished my hand into the top of my tank top and started tweaking a needy nipple, pulling and pinching, until that sweet bite of pain threw me over the edge of the cliff and I came hard into his unyielding and devoted mouth. Bowing my back against the chair, I pulled hard on his hair, burying his face in my pussy as the pleasure speared through me.

"Oh God, James!" I whimpered, definitely a fan of exhibitionism but still with a modicum of self-restraint and bashfulness. We were still docked and I was a tad worried people might hear us, so I kept my voice low, even though inside all I wanted to do was shriek my climax up into the cloudless sky. "Oh God, oh God, oh God!"

I pulled even harder on his hair and pushed up even more into his face, not caring if he couldn't breathe, not caring about anything but how good it all felt, how good he made me feel. The scissoring stopped, and his fingers pushed up hard and ruthless right on my G-spot, and that familiar sensation of having to pee hit me hard, like a sucker punch.

"Holy fuck!" I cried, unable to contain myself or control my volume any longer.

And then the orgasm that had been destroying me in an endless wave of euphoria took on a life of its own and came at me again in full force, pleasure upon pleasure upon pleasure as I closed my eyes and saw nothing but spots and flashes of light while the man between my legs just continued to feast.

It was never-ending. I was sobbing and begging him to release me, but he ignored my pleas, instead pumping harder and faster into my pussy, while blowing cool air on my swollen clit.

"No ... no more, James," I said with a mewl. "I ... I can't do anymore."

"One more, baby," he muffled, the tip of his tongue grazing my clit in just a whisper of a touch. My leg jerked, and I pulled on his hair until I could see his face, his hungry lips and strong sexy chin glistening with my release.

"No! No more, please."

He made a sexy little pouty face. "You're sure you can't go one more time?"

I swallowed and nodded, squinting against the blinding sun. "No more. I can't. I think my clit is going to fall off."

His chuckle stirred the butterflies in my belly, low and deep and whisky-thick, a manly laugh, a sinister laugh. He enjoyed tormenting me within an inch of my sanity, until tears streamed down my cheeks and my body trembled as if I'd just stuck my finger on an electric fence. The man was a sadist, and I was a masochist; he loved the torture, and I loved the pain. We were the perfect pair.

Standing up from his spot on the chair, he offered me his hand. "All right, fine, but I'm still hungry, so I'm not finished with you, Mrs. Shaw."

I went to stand up, but my legs were jelly, and I collapsed back onto the lounger, pulling him down along with me.

"Jesus Christ, you literally tongue-fucked me until I can no longer walk!"

Another laugh rumbled through him, followed by a swift and precise boob squeeze.

"That's the plan, *wife*. You'll be in a wheelchair by the time this holiday is over. Come on." He stood back up and then scooped me into his arms. "I still need to carry you over the threshold."

I t felt so good to be back under the ocean. We hadn't been diving in a while, not since Christmas, when we were in Belize on our private island. Yes, we *owned* an island! James, my sexy, eccentric millionaire husband, had bought me a tropical haven off Belize for my birthday a few years ago, and it quickly became our go-to place for rest and relaxation.

It was fully equipped with eight bungalows and gorgeous white, sandy beaches, and for the majority of the year, we rented out the cabins. But most Christmases, when the weather in the Pacific Northwest turned less than stellar, we packed up, ditched the cold and spent three glorious weeks in our bathing suits. My parents and James' parents usually followed us, and then, throughout the three weeks, various friends or other family members would come to visit as well.

But we wanted to go somewhere different for our honeymoon. We wanted to explore the world and see new and exciting dive sites. So after careful deliberation—it was between French Polynesia and the Mediterranean—we decided to rent a boat (well, it was more like a small ship) and set sail around the tiny little islands in the South Pacific.

It was just like riding a bike: getting on the gear, double-checking the equipment and walking like a drunk duck in the big, floppy fins. I was giddy to get back in the water and sink down into the deep.

We dropped anchor at the dive site known as Aquarium, a great first dive with a ring of corals, loads of butterflyfish, parrotfish, boxfish and colorful anemones. James had been meticulous in his research of all the major dive sites he wanted to visit. A dive instructor himself, he didn't see the need to hire a dive master to take us down but ended up ensuring that both our deckhands knew the area and dive sites anyway, just in case we wanted to employ their knowledge.

I fell madly in love with the juvenile cowfish and baby puffers as I always did, they were just so cute. I could have watched them for hours. James had spotted quite a few barracuda, and triggerfish, which we steered clear of, and I found two green moray eels slithering among the coral, as well as an octopus. The water was so clear and the visibility almost perfect that it was a shame we had to surface when we did. The forty-five minutes we were down there flew by, and I was disappointed that we had to head back up.

"Don't worry, princess," James chuckled, helping me remove my gear. "I have a night dive planned for us. So we'll have a quick dinner followed by a quick fuck, and then zip over to another site before we lay anchor for the night."

I shook my head. But he just grinned at me. The man was going to fuck me into a vegetative state before I even got a tan.

The night dive was something else. When we descended, I was immediately enveloped in pure and never-ending blackness. It was eerie and quiet, with only the sound of my own breathing and heart-beat to remind me that I was alive. James and I held hands as we submerged so that we would stay together. And before I could start to panic over the endless dark, the ebony sea was filled with bright light as James cracked a big glow stick and turned on his flashlight. I turned my light on as well, and suddenly things didn't seem so worm-holey, though we could still see only things right in front of our lights; every-thing else was eternal night and a tad spooky.

The longer we stayed under, the more my mind started playing tricks on me and I thought I was seeing creatures in the dark that weren't actually there. A few times I turned around suddenly, worried that a barracuda or shark was going to attack me from behind, but of course, nothing ever did. It was interesting to see all the different fish that came out at night, or how fish we saw during the day, rambunc-tious and full of pep, actually powered down and took a nap in their waterbed. I found myself chuckling several times as we perused the shelf reef and spotted several parrotfish snoozing away in a crevice or nook of rocks, safe from the current and any hungry predators looking for supper.

By the time we surfaced and stowed our gear, I was dead on my feet.

Completely wiped and it was only day one. It didn't help that we were dealing with jet lag, had hardly slept all night, and my husband's libido seemed to have shotgunned forty-seven Red Bulls before getting off the plane. So, I trudged my way down to the bedroom and schlepped my way into the bathroom, hardly able to keep my eyes open as I turned on the faucet for the shower.

I wasn't in there long before big, strong hands wrapped around my soapy body, caressing my breasts, and a growing erection pressed demandingly into my lower back. I turned around and faced my beautiful man.

"Well, hello there," I said in my sexiest voice, my tired eyes drinking in his rock-hard body.

"Hi." He started massaging my soap-covered breasts, pulling gently and then fiercely at my nipples. "Mmm, I love soapy boobies," he hummed. "They're so much fun."

"Mmm," I hummed in response, my body betraying my brain and responding in turn to his need.

"You tired?"

I sighed. "Exhausted."

His lips twitched as if he was trying to hide a smile. Dirty bugger.

I reached my hands down lower and started to softly stroke him. My lathered hands pumped him until he was standing straight up, the smooth purple head of his cock glistening in my palms. Leaning forward, I kissed the hollow beneath his strong jaw, feeling his heartbeat quicken. A moan fled from his parted lips when I nipped his chin, my own body thrumming with need as my breasts became heavy.

"Turn around, baby," he said gruffly.

Grinning, I spun around and bent over, using the wall of the shower to brace my arms and expecting a cock to spear me any second. But instead, my generous lover dropped to his knees behind me and lapped at my trembling folds, his tongue worshipping my wanton body as his lips kissed and sucked while his fingers pumped.

I was primed, wet and ready in no time, moaning and pushing into his face, riding the edge of euphoria like a skilled cyclist. And then, without warning, leaving my body drenched in longing, he stood up and immediately impaled me. I gave out a loud groan and curled my toes, letting my back sag like a saddle, feeling him hit me deep and hard, my whole body saturated with the sensation of being full and dominated by the powerful man behind me.

The water thrummed down on my back while James hammered me from behind, our feral sounds and the endless water filling my ears, drowning out even thought, so all I could do was feel and live in the moment. I slid my fingers down and started to make tiny circles around my clit, reaching back periodically to feel him—his length wet from me, disappearing inside of my body, only to emerge once more and then drive back home. My knees threatened to buckle from the force of his passion and the exhaustion of my body. Noticing my fatigue, he wrapped an arm around my waist to keep me standing, all the while never losing his cadence or his force. The man was a full-on sex machine.

I was so close, my release just beyond my reach. The man was an expert at withholding my orgasms from me, making me beg—he loved it when I begged. He knew exactly how to bring me almost there and keep me balancing on the precipice for ages, making the journey almost as good, if not better, than the destination.

Ready to come, I clenched my muscles around him and pushed back, taking as much of him inside me as I could, enjoying the sudden inhale and grunt from the beast behind me. He felt it, too, and his rhythm started to wane, which let me know he was riding the edge as well.

"I'm going to come," he groaned.

"Spank me!" I panted. "Hard!"

He made a rude noise in his throat, followed by a primitive growl.

"Oh God!" And then he smacked my ass cheeks six times repeatedly, each time a tad harder than the last, the fact that my butt was wet only making each whack sting just a little bit extra.

It was the last spank that did it, and I leapt off the cliff, free-falling in a delicate spiral down into the rabbit hole, while the world around me appeared to be nothing more than blurry white lights and diamonds in the shape of water droplets. I continued to fall, and then, seconds later, James found his release and fell with me. His moans echoed in my ear as my body milked him in ecstatic ripples, pulling him deeper and deeper down the rabbit hole with me while the water thundered around us like torrential rain and the steam enveloped us in its gossamer fog.

CHAPTER 4

I t was weird; we'd already spent one night (technically) as husband and wife, on the jet, but tonight felt like the first *real* night. The first *full* night. Perhaps it was James' apprehensions and his alarming reluctance to make love to me for fear of disappointing me, or that we didn't actually get to bed until nearly two or fall asleep until close to four, but whatever it was, it hadn't felt like our first night together. So I wore my "bridal" lingerie to bed tonight instead.

A sucker for satin, lace and a sexy print, I had a stash of bras, panties, and lingerie that rivaled Victoria's Secret and kept James with a constant half-chub and a stream of drool hanging down his chin. And although the scraps of expensive fabric spent more time on the floor than they did on my body, it didn't stop me from buying them or dressing up for my man.

I'd spent far too much time fussing over my outfit for the night as well. Probably more time than I had fussed over my wedding dress, because, for some reason, this outfit seemed more important. This was who we really were as a couple. No eyes on us, no expectations or judgment, just us. Hopelessly obsessed with each other and filthy as hell about showing it.

So after our shower I shooed James out of the bathroom and went to work getting dressed. Alyssa had helped me pick out the outfit. The two of us had gone to Seattle for a girls' weekend, where we spent the majority of our time shopping, and when we weren't shopping, we were eating. Seattle has a great food truck scene! I came back nearly five pounds heavier, but thankfully most of it wound up in my boobs.

After much deliberation and trying on dozens of outfits, I'd ended up going with a white, lacy push-up bra bodice, a matching white skirt (if you could even call it that? I think skirts are more than four inches wide), no panties (because why?), white thigh-highs and white fuck-me pumps that would probably never actually touch the ground. And then, just for dramatic flair, I covered it all up with a diaphanous, white, floor-length robe. It took me forever and a day to blow-dry my mermaid hair, but I wanted everything to be perfect.

"Stop right there, beautiful," James purred, as I stepped out of the bathroom and shut off the light.

The room was full of carefully lit candles (as the fire chief's daughter, I was always nervous around an open flame, and on a rocking boat, my heart rate jolted sky high), but seeing the uneasy shift of my eyes, James grabbed my hand and pulled me over to one of the candles.

"They're LED, Junior Fire Chief, don't worry, see." He held one up and put his finger into the faux flame.

I let out a sigh of relief, and he guffawed low in his chest.

"Always the worry wart."

"Noooo," I whined. "But an open flame on a rocking boat ... you're just asking for smoke on the water."

"And fire in the sky?" he asked with a carefree grin.

I rolled my eyes, but he took that as an invitation and reached for me again. I went to move into him, but he held me out at arm's length, his eyes raking my body and clearly liking what he saw. Meanwhile, he was wearing my favorite outfit of his, nothing but black boxer briefs with a noticeable tent, chin stubble and a smile.

"You are the most beautiful thing I've ever laid eyes on," he said quietly, his Adam's apple bobbing thick in his throat while his pupils dilated to near dinner plates and his lids drooped to half-mast.

I rolled my bottom lip between my teeth and averted my gaze, a flush of warmth creeping up my neck and into my cheeks and hairline. No matter how many years it'd been since my relationship with Tom had ended, I still didn't always feel as though I deserved such compliments.

My eyes traveled around the room and landed on his nightstand, where an impressive and arousing array of kinky toys and paraphernalia sat ready to use. I swallowed and licked my lips, the fatigue of the day suddenly forgotten, replaced with the all-consuming need to be taken.

His eyes followed mine, and he hummed softly while pulling me hard against him, spinning me around in the process. My back was to his chest, and I couldn't help but press my butt into his erection.

He cupped my chin with one hand and angled my neck to the side, running his nose and then his lips down the tender vein. I felt my nipples pearl against the lace of the bra, my breasts growing heavy and full of need. I closed my eyes and sunk into his warmth, letting him mould my body how he saw fit. I was his to do with as he pleased. I was his.

His free hand came up, and he cupped my breast, pulling on the tender bud beneath the fabric until I gasped from the snap of pain. I pushed back into his pelvis again and giggled at his groan of pleasure.

There were no more words. There didn't need to be. He peeled the sheer robe off my shoulders and let it fall to the floor in a pool of white quicksilver at my feet, while his hands began to roam and caress my skin until I was riddled with gooseflesh and trembling at the idea of the night to come.

He guided me back to the bed, where he spread me out in front of him, and then, just like last night, he stood back up at the foot and stared down at me. Only this time, instead of apprehension in his eyes, they were on fire, full of conviction and the desire to dominate and take.

My chest heaved against the strain of my bra. I was breathless, and I'd hardly even moved. I shifted on the bedspread; my butt cheeks were still a little tender from the shower, but the friction was a sweet reminder.

I watched him saunter over, all cocky male bravado, to the night-stand, where his eyes shifted across the lined-up toys. He hummed quietly to himself before reaching down and selecting something I didn't recognize. Kneeling up on the bed, he shuffled over to me, his big body hovering over mine, ready to tease, torture and turn me into putty.

Opening up his palm, he revealed a big roll of what looked like white elastic, the kind you might find in a fabric or craft store that gets used as a waistband for pants and such. It was about half an inch wide, and from the looks of things, he had several feet of the stuff.

"Have you heard of elastic band play?" he asked, reaching back onto the nightstand for some scissors.

I shook my head, my hair shifting around me.

"I'm going to tie the bands around various parts of your body, your arms, your legs, your stomach. It'd be cool if you'd let me tie one around your hips and up through your pussy, but I understand if you're not ready for that."

My wide eyes and sudden fervent swallowing must have made him say that last part. I was all for pain, all for a little slap and tickle, but elastic bands? On my clit? Ouch!

His mouth curved up into another salacious grin. "I didn't think so. Let's just stick to limbs and belly tonight, and if it's something you like, we can explore further another time."

I nodded, relieved that he wasn't going to be snapping my vagina with rubber bands anytime soon.

"But first ..." That sly smile was back. "You're wearing far too much clothing, wife of mine. And as hot as fuck as you look, I'm afraid this virginal outfit of yours ..." The twinkle in his eye told me he was having a hard time not laughing. It was true, I did look rather *virginal* in the lingerie, and lord knows I was anything but. Perhaps, in hindsight, the outfit should have been black. "... Is just going to end up on the floor in a matter of seconds. I want nothing between me and your body tonight, got it?"

I nodded again.

"But that doesn't mean I can't enjoy myself relieving you of these scraps." He set the roll of elastic and scissors to the side and started to slowly, ever so slowly, remove the stays and peel down my thigh-highs. He knew what he was doing; he knew that every delicate touch of his fingers sent a shard of need straight through my body and deep into my belly. That the way his big, warm, strong hands caressed my thighs, my calves, my feet, was pure sorcery. Like a trainer and a wild beast, he was subduing me, stroking me until all I could do, until the only choice I had, was to submit to him, fully and completely. Yield to his wishes, to his demands and let him ravish me.

I bowed my back and bit my lip as his fingers continued to roll the sheer fabric down my freshly shaved legs. He pulled the fuck-me pump off my foot and then tossed the thigh-high onto the floor.

"These stay," he said gruffly, and then he put the shoe back on my foot like a naughty knight in shining boxer shorts.

Next came the bodice. And unlike a normal bodice with the millions of hook and eye clasps in the back, this one boasted a discreet zipper on the side—easy on, easy off!

He had me naked in seconds, my chest heaving while my throat felt dry and my pussy was saturated. And then he went to work. Methodical and precise, like he was with everything, he'd wrap a strand of the elastic around my thigh to measure and then measure again before he cut.

A master craftsman in the woodshop, my man could make anything, be it an armoire, a bed, a table, or a naughty spanking bench that we pulled out on weekends. He was a pro. So to see him put the expertise of "measure twice, cut once" into play here, in the bedroom, made me smile.

He put two around each thigh, one around each bicep, one around my back and across my breasts, another around my stomach and then the final one lower across my hips so that it rested on the top of my pubic bone. By the time he was finished and I looked down at his hand-iwork, I felt more like a zebra than a blushing bride.

"God, you look sexy," he said with a growl. "So fucking sexy."

I licked my lips and looked up into his eyes. "Now what?"

"Now?" he leaned over to the nightstand again and grabbed a black sash. "Now I blindfold you so you have no idea where I'm going to strike or when." And then he wrapped the soft sash around my head until I couldn't see a thing.

"Everything okay?" he asked. "The elastics aren't too tight or cutting off circulation to anything vital?"

I shook my head. "Nope." But before I could even finish that one syllable, a snap of the band on my upper left thigh made me yelp. "Holy shit."

"How was that?"

"Fucking painful."

"On a scale of one to ten?

"An eight."

"On a scale of Stop Right this Instant an—"

But I cut him off. "Please ... more."

I didn't have to see him to know he was smiling. And then he obliged, this time to each of my arms. I hissed and squirmed on the bed as he plucked the cords wrapped around my body as if I were a harp, playing beautiful, naughty music against my flesh.

Each flick of the elastic was bloody painful. We all know what that feels like; it's not pleasant. But with each carefully timed pluck, my body fell deeper into arousal. The pain morphed into an all-encompassing heat that spread throughout my body and across my skin like wildfire. Every nerve ending was awake and alive and screaming for more.

I shifted my butt on the bed and felt wetness beneath me on the sheet while my nipples throbbed and my chest rose and fell in quick succession. The man hadn't even put his lips on me; he hadn't touched my breasts, my clit, my ass, nothing, and I was already hot and ready for him. Already so turned on, so tuned in that he could probably just pinch my clit and I'd explode right then and there.

The band across my breasts and pubic bone had to be the most painful. I remember when I used to get waxed. Everyone thinks the labia or anus are going to be the most excruciating part of your body to have the hair ripped from, but it's not, it's the pubic bone, and holy hell, did that elastic band smart.

"Could you come just from this alone?" he asked, his voice thick with strain. If I were to guess, I'd say the man had a pretty painful erection and was aching to be inside me.

"No," I said softly. "It feels good ... really, *really* good. But I want you."

I felt a dip on the bed, followed by a low growl above me. The vision flitted through my mind of a timid mouse who had just stumbled into a dark cave while the mountain lion, hidden in the shadows, slowly crept forward, licking his chops and ready to devour. I smiled. I was no timid mouse, but James was a lion, proud and virile, and he was certainly licking his chops, of that I was sure.

The intoxicating scent of my husband, woodsy and all-male, filled my senses, while the raw masculine heat of him radiated toward me in waves, loaded down with pheromones and lust. Lifting my hand up, I felt around for his face. It was inches above mine, hovering in wait until I realized he was there and welcomed him with my touch. I cupped his cheek and brought his lips down to mine. He hadn't said I couldn't move my arms; he hadn't really given me any instruction, so as far as I knew, all this was okay.

"I want you ... only you, from now until forever," I said against his mouth.

"Oh, Emma." And then his lips crashed against mine, and his tongue dove inside. Long, lascivious licks against my own tongue had me grinding thin air, searching for him, desperate for friction, desperate to feel him against me, inside me. But he denied me. He kept his body poised above mine, too high for contact, so all I got was his mouth.

I grappled at him with my arms, frantic to feel his weight on me, my nails clawing up his back while my legs looped around his hips and I fought to pull him down to me.

"Please ..." I begged against his torrid and relentless kisses. "Please ..."

He must have stripped at some point, because before I knew it, he had lowered himself down to me and was poised at the apex of my thighs. I lifted up to greet him, and he drove home.

"I want you on top," he said with a grunt, between brutish thrusts. "That way I can bite your tits and stick a finger in your ass."

I ran my tongue up the length of his neck. "Yes."

He wrapped an arm beneath me, and we started to rock, once, twice, three times to gain enough momentum, and then we rolled across the bed, still connected, until I was on top.

"I want to see you," I said as I started to move, feeling him languidly glide in and out of me. We were no longer in a rush, no longer frantic. The pleasure was building slowly, and we were going to enjoy our time together and make it last.

The sash fell away, and the dim light from the room overwhelmed my eyes. I blinked a couple times to adjust and then came face to face with my love.

"You're beautiful," he said softly, his hand coming up and twirling my hair around his fist. He tugged my head down until my lips hovered just above his. "You're my everything."

I swallowed, loving that dull ache in my skull from when he pulled my hair. "And you're mine."

"I love you."

A hot tear slid down my cheek, and he used the thumb on his free hand to wipe it away.

Emotion choked me as I stared down into my lover's eyes, into my husband's eyes. "I love you, too. From now until forever." I continued to move, bracing myself on either side of his arms and letting my breasts brush against the soft scattering of hair on his chest. Back and forth over his shaft I slid.

I hadn't noticed where his free hand had gotten to but was quickly reminded when two impish fingers plucked at the elastic on the back of my thigh and let it come down with a sadistic snap. I yelped against his lips but then started to giggle. The man knew how to keep me on my toes.

James started to laugh, too, and soon we were both chuckling softly while trying to kiss, our bodies still connected and shaking with controlled mirth.

His fist tightened around my hair, and he pulled until my lips reluctantly left his. I looked down into his cerulean eyes, so filled with love. Another snap of the elastic, this time on my back.

"Fuck!" My eyes flared, and he just grinned back at me. I lunged for his mouth with my teeth, but his fingers around my hair kept my head in place.

"Uh-uh, Mrs. Shaw," he tutted with a cunning grin. "I'm in control."

I growled. "Not anymore." And then I squeezed my muscles around his cock and picked up speed, riding him hard and fast again until the orgasm brewing inside my belly started to bang on the door and demand release.

His chuckle was low and deep, and I felt it against my chest. But instead of fighting me, he pulled my hair again until I was forced to rear up over him, then he dipped his head and latched firmly onto a needy nipple, drawing it into his mouth and lashing at it with his tongue. I inhaled quickly from the sudden rush of pleasure, *yes!* And then that free hand, that naughty free hand that liked to torment me and make me squeal, snuck down and around. Two inquisitive fingers drew my wetness up between my cheeks, probing my tender rosette and getting me good and ready.

My body was an inferno ready to combust and would do so in T-minus ten seconds. Hard and harder I rode him, crying out when his teeth clamped down around a diamond-hard bud and pulled, and then crying out again when those sneaky fingers pushed inside my anus and began to pump.

Seven ... six ... five ... the climax was there; I was so close. Blood pumped loud and quick in my ears while the scent of my man and our passion possessed my senses. Four ... three ... two ... I lunged forward once again and snagged James' bottom lip with my teeth, pulling like a savage beast, needing to consume him.

One! I detonated. Stars burst behind my closed eyes as the pleasure speared through me and took hold of my being. My clit throbbed against his pubic bone as he continued to buck up into me, searching for his own release. I squeezed him hard, drawing him deeper inside me, willing him to come.

The orgasm took hold of every cell of my body, every strand of my hair. And it seemed endless. A sob escaped me as I felt a second climax begin to unfurl, the first one having not even completely ended. And then just because he was a twisted fucker, my man plucked the elastic on my thigh again and pushed me over the edge one last time.

"Well, *wife*," James said, stalking out of the bathroom a few moments later, "I'd say that was a very successful new addition to our kinky lifestyle, wouldn't you say? I certainly liked it."

I looked down at my striped body and gave him a raised eyebrow. "I look like a zebra."

His mouth stretched into a cocky smile as he slid into bed and pulled the covers up to his navel. "Naw, not a zebra, a *tiger*. And a very sexy tiger at that."

Yawning, I reached over and turned off the light on the bedside table. "Yes, well, I'm not saying I didn't enjoy it, but I'm not sure I'll ever be cool with you snapping my clit with one of those torturous bands ... not unless I can return the favor to your favorite parts."

He turned off his own light and then leaned over to kiss me. "Not on your life, woman."

I started to laugh. "Hypocrite."

Grabbing me around the waist, he tucked me in close until we were spooning. "Damn straight. Now go to sleep. I plan on fucking you all day tomorrow, and I need you good and rested."

CHAPTER 5

The following afternoon I was busy emailing a few of my co-workers when James walked into the onboard office. He had that look in his eye. And despite how pressing the content of my email was, I couldn't deny the rush of longing that whizzed through my body from just one simple hooded look.

Just before the wedding I had been promoted to Director of Studies at the ESL school I worked for, so despite the fact that I was on holiday, on my honeymoon no less, problems still popped up, and I had to deal with them. This time it was a couple of Korean students who were refusing to pay for their last two semesters, even after we'd deferred their payments once because they told us their families had fallen on hard times. The bleeding heart in me had waived the penalty and said they could pay this semester, and they had been incredibly grateful.

But things started getting a little shady when they'd shown up to class in Prada and Gucci, went out for expensive lunches every day, and both of them continued to drive expensive Mercedes Benz, while the bling on their wrists and in their ears cost more than my parents' house. So Allan, my *gay-dian* angel, as he calls himself, and one of my best friends and co-workers, went all "Debt Collector" on them and confronted both boys.

Turns out, after Allan had done a bit of digging and asking around, that the boys had lied and had done this to other schools in the past. So now I was trying to troubleshoot the issue of recouping payment from their families back in Korea, while also trying to have a stress-free honeymoon. Needless to say, things were not going well, as their parents were not cooperating, denying that their boys would ever do anything wrong and refusing to pay. I was close to pulling my hair out strand by strand by the time my husband came in with sex in his eyes and a boner in his pants.

"Put the laptop down, sweetheart," James said, coming over to stand next to me, staring me down.

I shot him an irritated glare. Now was not the time for sexy times. I was busy. I had fish to fry and troubles to shoot. He could take his erection elsewhere, because at the moment, I wasn't interested.

"Now."

"I'm busy," I said through gritted teeth.

"I'm not asking ... *wife.*"

I rolled my eyes. This one was one of our role-play games. He wasn't *actually* this big of an ass, but sometimes we pretended that he was all Mr. Cocky-Dom-do-as-I-say, and I would drop whatever I was doing and then drop to my knees. Some days I loved it and fell to the floor willingly, but today was not one of those days.

"I'm busy," I said again. He went to reach for my arm, but I jerked it away, not even bothering to look up from the computer screen. "Fuck off ... please." A few seconds later, I dared to take a peek at the man above me.

Cobalt-blue eyes flashed fire for just the briefest of seconds, but I didn't care. I turned back to the computer screen. Allan said the boys were going to try and countersue us, for what he had no idea, but now we needed to get the lawyers involved. I needed to call Alyssa.

"Emma."

Letting out a big huff, I turned to face him. "What, James? Can't you see I'm busy? The whole school is going up in smoke, and I'm the only one that can put out the fucking fire. But instead I'm currently floating around the South Pacific in a hot pink bikini with a sex-god staring at me and demanding I ride him like a pony. Not right now, please?"

His face fell, and his mouth actually dropped into a pout. It was probably one of the most adorable and heartbreaking things I'd ever seen, and it made me feel like complete shit. But he said nothing and instead just turned around and left, closing the door quietly and leaving me in my bitchy funk.

I spent nearly the entire day in the office, only leaving to go and grab a bite and use the washroom. James had remained scarce, fishing with Ezra and then standing up in the wheelhouse and driving to our next mooring site, while Ezra helped his wife in the galley.

We ate dinner in awkward silence, the clatter of utensils against plates the only sound to fill the warm tropical air. And although I'd cleared up the problem at work the best I could for the time being, I'd have to see what kind of emails I woke up to the next day. I couldn't get myself out of my funk.

I felt terrible for how I had spoken to James earlier in the day. He was just trying to be a loving husband, wanting to do what couples do on their honeymoon, and I had been a snarky bitch, taking my work problems out on him when he didn't deserve it. By the time we went to crawl into bed, we'd hardly spoken at all, and things between the two of us were tense. But I was determined to go to bed on a high note. Determined to end the night off right—end the night with a *bang*!

Snuggling up close, I shot him a sassy grin over my shoulder and then hooked my left leg over his body and angled my torso away from his slightly, feeling around the front of his lap to see if he was hard.

"For you darlin'?" he purred. Always." He put his phone down and then his glasses. His gaze was scorching hot, caressing my face and then slowly meandering its way down my body and zeroing in my breasts. He flexed his erection in my palm and we both chuckled.

I grabbed him by the chin with my free hand and looked deep into his eyes. I'd never get tired of looking into that piercing blue. So much depth, so much love and passion. The man had so many layers. And even now, after all this time and that we were now married, I felt like I'd only just scratched the surface of James Shaw.

"I'm sorry I was such a bitch earlier," I said, swallowing past the hard lump in my throat. "Work is in turmoil right now, and they need me to troubleshoot, and, well ... I'm just sorry. I shouldn't have snapped at you like that."

He rolled over onto his side so that his cock was nestled perfectly at my core. "No worries, princess. You don't *always* have to be up for it. You're human, not a sex-robot. I just hate to see you so stressed, especially when you're supposed to be on vacation."

I wasn't even really wet, but I wanted him so badly, wanted to apologize so fiercely, I didn't care. I grabbed him by the base and started to wedge him inside. The flared crown of his penis spread open the lips of my sex as I slowly started to sink down. Taking in one luscious inch of him at a time.

"Well, I'm not stressed now. And I'm definitely 'up for it.'"

"No foreplay?" he asked.

I shook my head. "We don't always need it. Sometimes I just want to fuck you straight. Being next to you, in bed with you, watching your eyes travel the length of my body and fill with fire is enough to rev my engine."

His hand came up, and he started to twiddle my nipple. "I can get on board with that. Fuck, I can get on board with anything you want, as long as I get to bury my cock in your sweet little pussy. And for the record, just the *thought* of you, of your tits, your ass, your mouth rev my engine. I walk around most days with a half-chub. And when I sit at my desk and stare at your picture all day, it's all I can do not to run to your work and fuck you in the copy room."

I leaned forward and nipped his chin. "I'm the boss now, you *could* do that. Bang me like a drum in between my beginner and intermediate English classes. I *do* have a forty-minute gap."

A low but no less ferocious purr rumbled up through his chest and his eyes darkened. "Done. You won't even see me coming and I'll scoop you up and toss you up on top of the copier. Fuck you hard and deep. Would you like that? My cock ramming into your creamy little cunt as the light flashes beneath the glass, taking scans of your luscious ass?"

Hell yes! Oh God, the thought of it; the rhythmic sound of the copier, the smell of the ink, the smell of sex, the smell of James. I could see it now. Hear it in my mind. Feel it. I wanted it. I wanted that exact scene. I'd had him countless times in his office, blown him, fucked him, but we'd never had sex at my work. That had to change.

I licked my fingers and started rubbing rough circles around my clit. "Talk dirty to me, James," I said, my breath already coming out ragged from how good he felt inside me. "And I mean fucking filthy. I love it when you go all alpha and nasty. Or just shut up and kiss me."

His laugh was low and husky. "Such a bossy little horndog." But he did as he was told, and he reached for my head with his free hand and his lips crashed down on mine. I rammed my tongue into his mouth and started to twirl it around his. My whole body was suddenly caught up in this wild urge to fuck and to fuck wild. We hadn't had sex in this position in ages, and he was hitting inside me in a new way, plus my clit was completely exposed and eager for attention, as were my breasts. And both our hands were free, void of needing to support any kind of weight, so we could give my needy and greedy erogenous zones the attention that they deserved.

James slid his leg between mine and cupped my breast with his warm palm, pulling on it for leverage. The angle changed again, and he started hitting me deep inside, and in just the right spot.

I fiddled with my clit for a while, using my own wetness and saliva to bring myself close to the brink, sliding my fingers down to feel his thickness disappearing inside me with each thrust. But I wanted more. I wanted hot and filthy, forbidden and depraved. I gripped him by the base and pulled him out, angling him just a little lower so that he hit my soft rosette. I was so wet, so primed and so turned on, I knew there'd be no trouble or resistance. I sunk down onto him, pushing out my muscles to grant him access. He slid in no problem and, a second later, was buried deep inside my ass.

"Holy fuck!" he moaned. His hands continued to torment my breasts, plucking just a little harder and kneading just a little more firmly while my own fingers drew delicious circles around my hard and swelling clit.

I started to move, dropping my bottom down onto his shaft, loving the way he felt inside me. It was so dirty, so raunchy, but damn if it didn't feel amazing. My clit was growing harder and bigger by the second, and my breasts tingled and ached as he pinched and pulled. I was close to combustion.

"I ... I'm close," I panted.

"Me too, baby, me too. Fuck, your ass is so fucking tight."

"I ... oh God!" And then it claimed me. The orgasm swept through me like a cyclone, destined to destroy and decimate everything in its path. "Fuck, fuckity, fuck!" I cried, rearing up off the bed only to crash back down into the pillows, my fingers still furiously teasing my clit as it swelled and pulsed.

"Aargh!" James bellowed, pulling even harder on my nipples as his climax ratcheted through him. He snarled. "Best. Fucking. Wife. Ever!" Then he grabbed my hair and pulled my head toward him so his mouth could snag mine. He bit my lip before opening wide and making me do the same, nearly jamming his tongue down my throat, exploring the recesses of my mouth.

I was whimpering at this point, actually whimpering as the orgasm continued to ricochet around my body, hitting me in swells that never seemed to end, like a wave caught between two islands, with nowhere to go, back and forth, back and forth, until I was forced to pry my hand off my clit with my other hand in order to end the madness.

I closed my eyes for a second; I wasn't even drunk, but the room seemed to be spinning. Were we caught up in a whirlpool?

"You okay?" James asked, his voice hoarse and sounding as exhausted and drained as I felt.

"Better than okay." I grinned. "Your cock's in my ass."

"Damn straight it is, woman, and a mighty fine ass it is. I must say that was entirely unexpected, but fuck if I didn't love it."

I giggled. "I just had the sudden craving ... and you know me, when I want something ..."

"Like a dog with a bone?"

He slipped out of me, and I stood up and waddled off to the bathroom. "Yes," I called back. "A *bitch* in heat who wants her *bone* buried in every hole. Can you manage that?"

"Tonight?" he asked with a surprised tone. "You want me to fill all three holes tonight?"

He followed me into the bathroom and started washing his hands as I sat there peeing.

"Christ, woman, I fucked you like four times yesterday, not to mention that bit of sacrilege we just committed a minute ago."

I gave him a mock pout. "This coming from the man who is determined to put me in a wheelchair by the time we get home. I already had trouble walking this morning, I'd like to point out."

"Ah," he scoffed, "you were just finding your sea legs."

CHAPTER 6

A few days later, we moored just off the island of Moorea, which isn't too far from Tahiti. It took less than an hour to get there, and we weren't even giving 'er—pretty much just drifting with the waves while James trolled off the stern. With its jagged volcanic mountains looming high and mighty over pristine beaches and opulent resorts, the island is what postcards were made of. We laid anchor in a bay just in front of The Windward Hibiscus Hotel, and after a beautiful afternoon dive where we saw reef sharks and dolphins, we took the dinghy to shore to go and have dinner.

"I must say, *wife,* that you look particularly stunning this evening," James said as he jumped out and tied the small motorized boat up to the dock. "Is that a new dress?"

He helped me climb out, and for just a second I wobbled where I stood. Barely a week on the boat, and I'd already forgotten how to walk on land.

"It is, and thank you." I smoothed down the skirt of my plum-colored, jersey-knit dress and then pointed a toe in my cork wedges. "Where are all the other boats?" I asked as he took my hand and we started to make our way up the narrow dock.

He lifted one shoulder. "The resort is *very* private, and you're not allowed to dock here. It's for hotel guests only. But I called ahead and made some arrangements. They were cool with me taking the dinghy in but asked for us to leave the yacht in the bay. It's pretty shallow here and, among other things, this is an eco resort, so they didn't want to disturb the sensitive reef below."

I gaped up at him. "Really? You made *arrangements*?" It didn't matter that I'd been with the man for nearly three years, or that we owned an island; his immense wealth and the power it wielded still surprised me.

"Yeah. Believe it or not, but a buddy of mine that I went to school with owns the hotel. Found him on Facebook about a year ago, and we've been chatting. Told him our honeymoon plans, and he said for me to let him know if we were in the area and he'd hook us up." His mouth drew up into a big smile as his eyes looked forward to a figure coming toward us on the grass. I followed his gaze. "Ah, and speak of the devil." He stuck his hand out. "Tate, how goes it, man?"

He was handsome, boy, was he handsome. Tall, dangerous and drop-dead gorgeous didn't even begin to describe the man in front of me, whose muscles threatened to rip out of his light blue dress shirt and whose eyes were as green as the mountains behind him. If I wasn't already married to the sexiest man on the planet—yeesh, this guy was a clear runner-up for sure!

"James, buddy, long time no see." He took James' hand, and the two shook for a couple of seconds, but then Tate's eyes fell down to me, and the smile that stretched across that impeccably groomed stubbly face made my knees turn to jelly almost instantly. "And this must be the lovely Emma?" He stuck his hand out and I took it. It was big and firm and warm. Holy Hannah, this man was hot!

"Hi," I said shyly. "You have a lovely resort."

Green eyes flashed intrigue and, if I wasn't mistaken, maybe an ounce of need, or was that jealousy? I couldn't tell. But he quickly recovered and then turned back to James while making sure to keep me included in the conversation.

"Thank you. Yes, she is rather beautiful, isn't she?" Tate motioned for us to turn and follow him. Soon the three of us were wandering across the well-groomed grounds toward the main hotel area among palm trees and vegetation galore, while the chirp and warble of tropical birds filled the balmy night air.

"How's the trip so far?" Tate asked, his big body next to mine making me a tad nervous. A man hadn't winded me like this since I'd met James. What was it about him that made my stomach go all aflutter?

James nodded. "Good, good. No rough waters, great dive conditions, good fishing spots. Thanks for recommending Ezra and Lola. They've been awesome so far."

"You're welcome. I only recommend the best, and for friends, the best of the best."

I swallowed. "So, uh ... how long have you owned the resort, Tate?"

His eyes zipped back down to me, and he smiled. "Oh, about six years now. It was a rundown little three-star when I got my hands on it. Got it for a steal, too. And now I've turned it into one of the most elite and prestigious resorts in French Polynesia."

"Wow! That's amazing. Congratulations!" was all I could think of to say, squeezing James' hand almost a little too tight and moving closer to him. He probably wasn't doing it on purpose, but Tate's big, muscular arm was grazing my shoulder and making me uncomfortable.

"Thanks." He grinned again. And then I watched as his eyes traveled down the length of my body, from my hair to my toes and back, lingering just a fraction too long on my breasts.

James caught his eyes and grunted. "Dude, cool it. I don't share. Tone it down."

My eyes went wide, and I spun my head around to look up at my husband. Meanwhile, Tate just burst out laughing. "All right, fair enough, man. But I'm allowed to appreciate beauty when I see it, right?"

My face was pure fire.

"Of course. My wife is fucking gorgeous, and men can check her out all they want. In fact, it turns me on a little to see the jealousy in the poor fucker's eyes when I grab her like this and kiss her." And then he did just that. He stopped us in our tracks, swung me around and dipped me low, his mouth devouring my gasp.

I heard Tate chuckling beside us. But I couldn't help myself; my husband was an aphrodisiac incarnate, and I was drawn to him. My hands found their way to James' shoulders, and I parted my lips, letting his tongue dip in, challenging mine to a dance-off.

"Uh ... guys, we have reservations," Tate said, still laughing.

James finally pulled his lips from mine. "It's okay. I know the owner."

Tate continued to laugh.

James helped me stand, only I couldn't quite get a steady footing. The man's kisses had made me dizzy, and I stumbled into him. Big, strong hands came up under my arms, and then my feet left the ground.

"Do I need to carry you, *wife*?" he asked. "We haven't even been drinking."

I beamed up at him. Though I'm sure my face was as crimson as the setting sun, it certainly felt as hot.

"*You* make me drunk, *husband*," I said, motioning for him to put me down. He set me back on my feet, but then his hand fell to my butt, and he gave it a quick squeeze.

We fell back in line with Tate, and the three of us began walking again.

"Anyway ..." Tate said with a chuckle. "Fine by me, man. But you are right. Emma, you are beautiful. You're a lucky man, James." A shadow passed across Tate's face, lingering in his eyes for a moment or two before he caught me watching him and flashed me a big, sexy smile. He held the door open for us, and we walked into what can only be described as Oceanian opulence to the nth degree. Through the restaurant we walked, past tables of happy diners with big fruity tropical drinks of decadence in front of them, while a flame from a big grill in the center of the space randomly flew up to the rafters. The smell of fresh fish wafted through the air, making my stomach grumble.

The main restaurant was styled to look like a traditional Samoan or French Polynesian house, with a domed roof and evenly spaced posts supporting the beams. I wondered if it was thatched with the traditional sugarcane leaves, or if they'd decided to go with something a little more modern.

Tate led us out onto the deck where it was more of a lounge-style atmosphere, with wicker chairs and tiki torches everywhere, while a breathtaking panoramic view of the bay and the sinking sun welcomed us. James pulled out my chair, and Tate signalled for a waiter.

I let out the breath I'd been holding. "Wow, I can see why you live here. This is extraordinary."

Tate's eyes danced emerald fire as he smiled at me. "It is, isn't it?"

I hadn't even been given a chance to order a drink, or even my meal, but somehow within seconds of sitting down, a funky-looking cocktail was placed in front of me, complete with a little umbrella and a wedge of pineapple. Moments later, the most decadent-looking barracuda steak I could have ever imagined was set before my hungry eyes.

"I hope you guys don't mind, but I ordered for us," Tate said, nodding and thanking the waiter, who was obviously going out of his way to make sure nothing at Tate's table was amiss.

"Not at all, man, this looks great. Thanks," James said, lifting his beer in a toast. The three of us clinked glasses, and then I dove into my fish. It melted in my mouth like succulent meaty butter.

I was too caught up in my food to pay any attention to the men, but when James said, "Right, babe?" I was drawn from my savory reverie and forced to join the conversation. Dear lord, the fish was good.

"What was that, sorry?"

Tate grinned that nipple-pebbling smile again, his brown brows bobbing ever so slightly. "James was just saying that you're having some problems at work right now."

I took a sip of my drink. It didn't taste boozy, but I'm sure that was just because the bartender was an expert. Either way, it was good, and I wanted another. "Yeah, unfortunately. As I'm sure you know, as I'm sure you *both* know, being the big boss comes with its share of problems. Your time is never *really* yours when there's a crisis."

"Anything I can help with?" Tate asked, taking a casual swig of his beer.

I gave him a weird look. Why and how could he help? The problem was back in Canada; we were here, and I hardly knew the man. What a weird question.

James' hand landed on my thigh, and he gave it an affectionate rub. "Sorry, babe, I should have mentioned: Tate speaks Korean. He lived there for a while, did a year abroad, and he does a lot of business with Koreans. Right, man?"

Tate nodded. "I'm fluent in Korean if you need me to translate or call or write an email for you. If the language barrier is part of the problem."

I gaped at him. Holy shit. This man may have just saved me, saved the company and saved my honeymoon. I grabbed my purse and reached inside for my phone, pulling up the emails and the phone numbers of the family of the students. I handed my phone to Tate. He punched the number into his phone, asked me to bring up the email correspondence I'd been having with Allan on my phone, and then he picked up both phones and wandered off to a more secluded part of the restaurant, the phone to his ear and his lips moving.

My head swiveled around to James, and the grin on his face was enough to make me want to tear off his linen shirt and toss him down on the table and ride him like the prized stallion that he was.

"You cunning, sexy demi-god," I said, shaking my head.

"Demi-god? Woman, I'm a full god."

I laughed but then nodded. "And cocky."

"Tate's a good guy, Em. He comes on strong, isn't shy about showing his interest, and that's gotten him into a fair bit of trouble in the past. But he's harmless. And when I emailed him about your problem, he offered to help. Even if he can't, I'm sure you'll be no worse off than before. And at least now, he can maybe clear up a few things that have gotten lost in translation."

I dug back into my fish, loath for it to get cold, though I'm sure it would still taste like heaven in a lime and herb sauce, even cold. "I hope so," I said, shoving the food into my cheek. "How come I've never heard you mention him before?"

His mouth split into a big, rueful smile. "Uh, well ... Tate and I *were* friends. And we *are* friends. But I may have punched him in the face when I found him in bed with Amy one night."

My jaw dropped, and my fork clattered to the plate. His smirk was huge as he nodded, apparently proud of his barbarian behavior, meanwhile I was hoping for answers.

He could tell I wasn't impressed, his lips twisted sheepishly. "We were all back from university for winter break," James went on. "Tate went to UBC with Justin and I, though he majored in something else, maybe marketing or international relations or something, I can't remember. Anyway, Amy was seventeen but still in high school, and Tate is a year or so younger than me, I think he was maybe twenty-two, but I caught him coming out of her room late at night, and I lost it. Hauled off and decked him. And then, well ... we kind of *lost* touch."

I shook my head. "That was a bit rash, don't you think? Considering you've nailed nearly every one of your sister's friends? And she's convinced you slept with her baseball coach, too."

The corner of his mouth twitched, but he didn't say anything. "Yes, well, perhaps. But she was ... *is* my baby sister, and I'll do anything to protect her. He wasn't the first guy I kicked the crap out of after finding them leaving her room. But, yes, perhaps it was. But Tate's forgiven me, I've forgiven him, and it's all good."

I gave him a wry look. "If you say so."

He tipped his beer up and waggled his eyebrows at me, my heart doing a happy little *pitter patter* from just how relaxed and playful he was. "I know so."

Seconds later, Tate joined us back at the table, and he was all smiles. "Ah, well, that was interesting."

Reluctantly, I put my fork of decadence down. "What? What happened?"

"The phone number your students gave you was *not* to their parents. It was to some friends back home. The little punks feigned ignorance and tried to give me the runaround, but finally, after much *cajoling* and threatening to call in a few *favors* from various friends of mine in Seoul, they gave up the goods, and I was able to call the real parents and relay the issue. They were devastated, to say the least, and very apologetic and will be wiring the money to the school shortly."

"Holy shit!" A few older guests shot me dirty looks, so I brought my volume down and offered them a very Canadian apology. "Holy shit!" I whispered. "You're a magician."

Tate drained his beer bottle and gave me a shrewd grin. "I've been called worse."

James just rolled his eyes. "Thanks, man. We really appreciate it. Now my wife can stop fretting about work. She doesn't have to lock herself in the onboard office any longer and can fuck me when I ask."

Tate snorted while I felt my cheeks get hot again, and I choked on the straw and drink that were currently in my mouth. No matter how much exhibitionism we'd engaged in over the years, or how much I enjoyed talking about sex with others, it still startled me when James brought it up. Normally the man was so quiet. He must really trust Tate to let his guard down so much.

"No worries," the brown-haired Adonis said, thanking the waiter for his second beer.

We spent the rest of dinner chatting amicably about various things, only to then have our conversation drowned out for a brief but entertaining twenty-minute show of traditional Polynesian dancers, complete with headdress, grass skirts and leis. By the time the dancers left, my meal was done, my drink was done, and the sun had set completely behind the horizon, leaving us with a black sky full of endless twinkling diamonds.

"So ... uh, any girlfriend or special lady in your life, Tate?" I asked, after I'd practically licked the plate clean of my meal and was now enjoying a refreshing and delicious coconut and pineapple gelato.

He shook his head. "No, I don't really have time. This is a busy job, and I live here at the hotel. So besides guests and staff, I don't really have time to meet anyone."

I made a pouty face. "That's too bad."

"That's not to say I don't enjoy the companionship of various women who give me the time of day, guests only though, I don't sleep with my staff. But as far as anyone *special* goes, no."

James made a rude noise in his throat. "You still swing?"

Tate grinned over the rim of his beer bottle. "When I can, but I haven't in a while. Wound up getting a little messy. Women wanted to leave their husbands for me. I'm just as content sleeping with one woman as I am three or four."

"Oh, swing? Like Justin and Kendra used to?" I asked, wondering why I wasn't feeling the effects of my drink at all. I was on my third coconut of the frothy drink, and I didn't even have the booze legs. My head was clear, and my feet were fine. Were the drinks just really weak? Or had the bartender gotten his wires crossed with another table and was serving me virgins?

Tate's eyebrows disappeared beneath the swath of chestnut hair that tumbled down over his forehead. "Justin swings now?"

James rolled his eyes. "His wife is a free spirit, and the two dabble and go to parties."

"Not so much anymore, though," I said. "Not since they had kids. I don't think they've been to any since Chloe was born."

Tate nodded. "Cool. But not you two?"

James shook his head. "I don't share."

Tate just snorted. "You never did. Though to be fare, if I had someone as gorgeous as Emma, I don't think I'd share her with another man either. It's easy to dabble and swing when you're unattached, but I think if I found 'the one' I'd be equally possessive and want to keep her all to myself."

"Damn straight," James said solemnly, his hand landing the top of my thigh, warm and inviting, making my whole body spark to life. He squeezed gently, and then a long, nimble finger stretched out and grazed my mound. Even with the layer of fabric between us I still felt his touch. My nipples tightened and I squeezed my legs together. He knew exactly what he was doing, and his low chuckle proved he was enjoying torturing me.

I swallowed. "Anyway ..." I said, looking down into my empty gelato bowl and wondering if I could get away with using my finger to wipe up the dregs. "Thank you again for helping me out, Tate. I really appreciate it. And if you're ever back in Victoria, please come and look us up."

I shot my husband a look that said, "Take me back to the boat and have your way with me," he read me loud and clear, removing his hand from my leg and pushing his seat back so abruptly it skidded across the wooden floor in a noisy screech.

Tate's eyes drifted down my body again, and he just smiled. "I will definitely do that, though I'm pretty much living the dream right now, so I can't say I'll be heading home anytime soon."

James pulled my seat out for me, and I stood up.

"Dreams are wonderful, but they're called dreams for a reason. They're not meant to last forever. You can make your reality pretty fantastic too ..." I said, giving my husband a loving look.

He returned it in kind, his eyes sparkling. "We certainly have."

"**N**ot another step, princess," James purred, later that same night, as I padded out of the washroom on bare feet, pick-combing my hair and letting it fall over my shoulders in rippled waves.

He was standing beside the bed, wearing nothing but black boxer briefs and a sinisterly sexy smile. "Drop the comb and take off your dress." His voice was calm but firm; my man definitely had a well-thought-out plan for tonight.

A shiver of anticipation ran through me as I did as I was told, letting the comb fall to the floor in a clunk and then slowly peeling the straps of my nightdress over my shoulders.

"Now touch yourself. Right there, don't move." I had taken a step with the intention of going over to the bed. "Pretend your hands are me; show me what you would do if I wasn't around."

"Well, normally I'm not standing up when I fuck myself," I sassed. "I prefer the comfort of a bed."

I didn't quite understand where he was going with this whole thing, but that didn't stop it from turning me on. My nipples ached—they were already so hard—while my cleft pulsed and my breasts felt full and needy.

"Don't challenge me. Just do as I ask. That little bit of insubordination, my love, has earned your pretty little ass ten smacks. Now come over here."

Oh, so this was the game we were playing tonight; I felt my heart skip and dance. He was going to be his uber-sexy, dominating self, and I was to submit and listen and obey and reap all the orgasmic benefits. I walked toward him, and he sat down on the edge of the bed.

"Bend over my lap."

My eyes went wide. I'm not sure he'd ever spanked me like this before. I was always on all fours, on the spanking bench, straddling him, or on my back with my legs in the air. This was new. "You want to spank me like a *child*?"

His lips turned up into a wicked grin as he reached for my hand. "Ain't nothin' childish about what I intend to do to you, princess. Trust me." I held out my hand, and he pulled me over his lap. Caressing my cheeks, rubbing his hands over my soft, shower-fresh skin, he prepared my body for the punishment to come.

"I'm not going to hurt you, but this is where we're going tonight, okay? I want you to touch yourself, bring yourself to climax, and I'm going to watch. And it's also a huge test for me, to see how long I can watch you touch yourself before I have to touch you, too. Before I can't take it any longer and I have to fuck you. I doubt you'll require punishment again after this, but if you beg for me, I will spank you. Do you understand?"

"I understand, and yes, I'm okay with this." My body trembled in his lap, eager and nervous about the first spank to come.

"Good. Now relax. You're shaking like a frightened kitten." He continued to massage and run his hands around and along my back and butt, bringing all the blood to the surface of my skin and awakening my nerve endings, which were ready and willing to join the party.

Eventually, my body calmed and I melted into his lap, putty in his strong and skilled hands. It was then that the first spank came, hard and fast on my right cheek, dead center, where all the meat and muscle is. I yelped, squirming in his lap, feeling his erection press against my belly.

"Stop wiggling, Emma. You're making it hard for me to concentrate. That's one."

Another smack came down, with what I could have sworn was a whistle in the air, rapid-fire speed and a cracking noise, landing square on the left one. I yelped again; tears stung the corners of my eyes, and a sudden sob escaped me. It wasn't overly painful. James was good at what he did, but the initial smack was a shock to the system. "God, your skin is beautiful; it gets such a sexy pink glow to it. Are you okay?"

"Yes." I was panting like a bitch in heat, surprised by how easily I managed to get out of breath from just two smacks. My core clenched while my body was humming for more. I could feel myself getting slick between my legs.

"Are you wet, baby?"

"Yes."

A finger grazed over my swollen cleft. "Jesus fuck, Emma. Your pussy is so swollen, so shiny. I'd give anything to slip my fingers inside you right now."

He gave out a groan and thrust his boxers-covered, fully erect cock into my pelvis. I pushed down, desperate to deliver just an iota of the torture he was giving me. He moaned again, following with two quick and hard smacks to each of my cheeks.

I squeaked and squirmed on impulse, relishing the warmth that spread from my backside into the rest of my body. He continued to spank me, varying his speed, the strength, and the location of his strike, keeping me on my toes and always guessing. I was breathless and damn near insane with arousal as I felt my pussy drip onto his lap.

"That's eight and nine. One more to go. Do you prefer a cheek?"

I growled a "No" before digging my nails into his calf, stanching the need to grind my pelvis against his thigh.

"All right, my choice."

He delivered the final deliciously painful blow to the left. Immediately after, he began planting soft, feather-light kisses all over my backside, numbing the sting but increasing my desire by tenfold.

"Your ass is perfect," he hummed, his lips buzzing against my skin. "So plump and soft and round, and perky as hell when you wear those tight black yoga pants."

I wriggled in his lap as he continued to kiss and nip my bottom, shamelessly humping his cock against my stomach while grinding my pelvis against his thigh. Was this part of the game? Because this was not how I got myself off, as much as I was enjoying it.

"Now, unless you'd like another spanking, I suggest you stand up and start showing me how you touch yourself. I'll tell you when you can get onto the bed."

He helped me up and then grabbed me by the shoulders, placing me six feet in front of him. He stepped back and reclaimed his spot on the edge of the bed, his trouser snake fighting desperately to be freed from its cotton prison. I smiled when I saw him let out a heavy sigh and pull his boxer briefs down, allowing his erection to bounce free and slap against his taut belly.

Fuck, he was stunning. You'd never know to look at him, with his honed muscles, rippled and defined, and that eight pack torso, that the man was forty. Yes, forty! I swallowed the lump in my throat, my tongue a sudden sand pit as the moisture in my body pooled warm and slick between my legs.

"You may begin," he said, with a comic hand gesture. "If you need a jumping-off point, maybe you should begin with your breasts."

"Okay ..."

Rolling my bottom lip between my teeth, I started to caress myself, massaging the heavy weight of my breasts with both my hands, running soft circles around each nipple with the pads of my thumbs, flicking and rolling until the hard peaks were red and achy. I licked my fingers and then continued to fondle myself, feeling them grow heavier as my need for climax increased.

I slid one hand slowly down my body, across my belly, and gently patted my labia with four fingers, moaning in delight as a jolt ricocheted through me from the first dose of attention delivered to my throbbing clit.

I lifted one eyebrow at him. "This may take a while. Not that I get myself off anymore, but I used to just bust out the ol' vibrator to get me there."

A thick whisky chuckle rumbled through him. "Not this time, baby. Take all the time you need."

My eyes closed and I continued to fondle myself. One hand gently smacking my cleft while the other one continued to pinch and tug on my tender nipples. My breasts throbbed from how heavy they'd become, aching for relief, for James to cup them and relieve the strain and pull of gravity. I tried my best, pawing and cupping but it just wasn't the same as my husband's big palms. Letting out a frustrated sigh I went back to plucking, loving how each pinch of my thumb and forefinger sent a rush of need directly to my clit, making it pulse and swell against my slapping fingers. I was caught up in the moment and starting to get into it when I remembered that James was watching me; I'd actually forgotten that he was in the room. I slowly fluttered my lashes open and found his eyes riveted to the sight of me pleasuring myself. Unblinking he watched me with wild and awestruck fascination.

His eyes were searing, pure sex, heat and hunger, a full-on inferno as he drank me in. One hand rhythmically stroked his heavy length as he continued to sit there on the edge of the bed, his elbows on his thighs, back hunched, leaning forward and gaping at me. A luminous bead of pre-cum emerged on the crown of his shiny cock, and I ached to lick it off. But I didn't even want to think about how many smacks that would cost me.

Or did I?

I watched him with my own fascination, his vulnerability and how he handled himself in private and brought himself to climax, open for me to see. It wasn't just me on display. He'd made sure of it. He was revealing just as much as I was. It was fun, erotic and wickedly dirty, and I found myself getting more and more into it, hypnotised by the rhythmic pumping of his fist over his veined length.

"Is this okay?" I asked, batting my eyelashes at him while pushing two fingers between my folds, drawing rhythmic circles around my nub.

He growled low, "Fuck, yes." Nodding slowly with a gulp.

I continued to tease and flick my nipples and breasts, loving what it did to him, but also relishing how good it felt. I loved my breasts. They were big, not quite identical in size, and they hurt when I ran without an industrial-strength bra, but they have always been my best feature. Even when I was overweight, had acne and braces and didn't know what the hell to do with my hair, I could still look in the mirror while wearing my bra and be like, "Well, you may be an ugly duckling, but at least your tits are nice."

James ordered me to move to the bed. Once positioned in the middle of the pillows, I quickly got back to task, trailing one hand down between my folds and inserting two fingers into my quivering pussy. I was drenched. I could feel my wetness running down my inner thighs as my fingers slid around my cleft with unimaginable ease. I scissored them back and forth and whimpered softly when my middle finger reached that almond-shaped softer tissue, the enigmatic and ever-puzzling G-spot. I brought my other hand down and started stroking gentle and soft circles around my clit, watching him with wanton eyes.

James was having a harder time with this than I was. There was a thin layer of sweat on his brow and upper lip, and he looked physically pained to be holding his own climax off for this long. He had swivelled his body around and was now sitting cross-legged at the foot of the bed, eyes wide, while his breath came in short and ragged pants.

When I was on my own, I was incapable of getting off with just vaginal stimulation—clit-stim all the way! But I much prefer the tongue or cock of a man to get the job done. Preferably the tongue and cock of the man whose tongue was hanging out of his mouth at that moment like a hound dog and whose thick and throbbing cock looked about ready to explode.

"Are you okay?" I asked, tilting my head forward on the pillows to get a better look at him.

"I'm fine." He swallowed, looking anything but. "This is so fucking hot. And way harder than I thought. All I want to do right now is shove my cock inside you and explode. Are you close?"

"No." I shook my head and whimpered, enjoying the touch of my own hands but craving the weight of his body pressing me into the mattress. Why was he torturing the both of us when we could just fix the whole thing by smashing our bodies together and fucking each other silly?

I continued to pleasure myself, inserting a third digit and delivering biting smacks to my clit with the tips of my other fingers. I was finally starting to get close; starving for an orgasm, my labia were beginning to swell, and my clit was growing larger and harder and increasingly sensitive. I went back to tiny circles, and with a soft cry and a few appeals to a higher power, I came.

My head rose off the pillows and all my muscles went rigid while my toes curled until I got a Charley horse as I continued to push and thrust my fingers into my trembling cleft, pressing hard on my G-spot inside but not quite managing enough pressure. The blood in my ears pumped heavily, drowning out all other sound and I continued to spiral up, up, up into sweet oblivion.

Seconds later, I fell back down to reality, my sex ultra-sensitive, so I pulled my hand away, my digits slippery with my arousal. Ordinarily I wouldn't have licked them off, but I knew that it would send James over the edge, so I sucked my fingers clean, tasting my own salty wetness.

"Holy fucking Christ." Lunging forward with a snarl, he impaled me in one swift thrust, coming immediately inside me, exploding his load and biting my shoulder to muffle his profanity-riddled cries.

I softly ran my fingernails over his back and butt, tickling him, welcoming him back down to reality in the gentlest way I could, his skin rising in gooseflesh beneath my fingers. "Well, that was hot."

His chest heaved as he pressed the full weight of his body into mine, trembling softly in the aftermath of his orgasm.

"That was so hot, but fucking torture." He licked my neck and bit my earlobe, making me yelp. Then he rocked us three times, lacing our legs together and rolling us over so that I was on top. His cock was still fairly hard and nestled deep and safely inside me. He shook his head. "I learned a lot, but we'll never do that again. I almost exploded. Does it normally take you that long to get off on your own?"

"Yeah." I shrugged. "Generally, when I don't have a vibrator. I'm a tough nut to crack. With a vibrator it's a bit quicker, but not much. You know how to get me close faster than anyone, including myself. I don't know why you thought you needed to observe me getting off. You're exceptional at what you do."

He nuzzled his nose against mine. "I just thought we'd try something different. But all I wanted to do was touch you. That was one of the hardest things I've ever done."

"Well, your cock looked like one of the hardest things I'd ever seen. I can only imagine what kind of a load you blew."

"Go pee, push it all out, come back, and then sit on my face. I want to see if I can get you off faster than you can."

"Okay!"

CHAPTER 7

We were a few weeks into the trip now, and besides my random afternoon of snarkiness early on, we hadn't hit a snag, bump or even a pebble in the road ... or I guess, in this case, on the open ocean. Things were going swimmingly ... ha ha, good one, Emma, and James and I were deliriously happy and so in love. The man seemed determined to fuck me until I was comatose, so all in all, we were having a great time.

I can't actually tell you what day of the week it was, or even what time it was, but I'm guessing it was midafternoon on roughly a Sunday and I was up on the top deck with my tablet. I'd been snap-happy on our last dive and was eager to send the awesome manta ray pictures I'd taken to my family and friends.

"Care to explain what the *FUCK* these are?" James asked, coming to stand next to me, clad in nothing but a pair of swim shorts. The way the sun shone on his skin made my jaw drop and my nipples tighten.

"Tic Tacs," I said sarcastically. "What do you think they are? It's my birth control. You've seen me take it hundreds of times. What the hell is going on?"

His mouth opened and closed and then opened and closed again, and he immediately reminded me of the whale shark we'd seen a couple days before, skimming along the surface with its mouth agape, trolling for lunch. He clamped his jaw shut and gnashed his molars together while his nostrils flared. The man was pissed. Why was he pissed?

"Why are you pissed?" I finally asked, removing my sunglasses and shielding my eyes with my hand.

"Why the fuck are *these* things here?"

I gave him an incredulous look. What the hell was with the rhetorical questions?

"So I don't get pregnant. What is going on here?"

"I thought you were going to ditch the pills and we'd start trying on this trip!" he finally said, waving the package around so flippantly I thought he was getting ready to toss them overboard.

I shook my head. "I never agreed to that."

"Yes, you did!"

More head-shaking. "No, I didn't, James. You were spouting off to everyone the day before the wedding that we were going to start trying on the honeymoon, and I never agreed to anything. I said, 'We'll see, but I wouldn't mind waiting to start trying in the spring.' Not once did I say, 'Yeah, knock me up, baby.'"

"So you don't want to have children with me, then?" His eyes were darting around the deck like a lost lamb's while he hinged at the hips so he loomed over me in an intimidating power position.

The man was an alpha in his industry and used to saying "jump" and his employees saying "how high." He didn't *need* to use intimidation techniques, because he simply *was* intimidating. But that kind of stance sent up red flags for me, and I immediately pushed myself up to standing. And then, just for good measure, I climbed up onto the lounge chair so that we were eye to eye.

"I never said that! I *do* want to have children with you."

"Then why are you still on the pill?"

My fists bunched at my sides. "Because I don't want to have children *yet*! We *just* got married. I'd like you all to myself for a bit, if I may?"

He shook his head. "I want to start trying now."

"Tough shit, Shaw. My body, my choice. I'm not ready."

"So what, you're just going to *withhold* my children from me?"

Oh my f-ing God! For a brilliant man, he could sure be dim at times.

"I can't *withhold* children from you if I don't have any in me. Where the fuck is this coming from?"

"I've been fucking you until you pass out every day for the past three weeks hoping ... thinking that I was getting you pregnant on at least one of the attempts. Only to find out it was all for naught."

"FOR NAUGHT!" I tossed my hands on my hips to keep myself from pushing him overboard. "You were only having sex with me to get me pregnant? Not because you love me and want to have sex with me?"

"Well, okay ... not for *naught*. I love fucking you. But I thought I was getting you pregnant, too."

"I'm diving," I said absently, at a loss for anything else to say; the man had me completely gobsmacked. "I shouldn't be diving if I'm pregnant."

He shook his head. "I talked to the doctor, and he said it was fine. You'd be so barely pregnant it shouldn't matter."

"You spoke with *my* doctor?" The slowly building anger inside me tasted bitter on my tongue.

"No, mine. But they're all the same."

And then it all started to make sense. I had thought that the reason there was no alcohol on board was because we were doing so much diving and didn't want to get ill. It hadn't occurred to me that James had decided to make our honeymoon a dry one because he expected me to be pregnant at some point. Had he spoken with the bartender at the restaurant back on Moorea too? Were those drinks virgins? He was also being extra attentive and nurturing (not that he wasn't anyway), but the foot rubs and massages had tripled, and the healthy eating, dear God, a person can only eat so much spinach before they turn into freaking Popeye. He'd been pumping me full of folic acid, and I didn't even know.

"This is not cool, man," I finally said, my head feeling like it was going to detach from my neck, I'd been shaking it so much. "I am not ready to get pregnant, and here you've been secretly turning me into a fucking Grade-A incubator."

"No," he said matter-of-factly. "We agreed on this." He seemed utterly convinced that we'd sat down and had a long chat about when we were going to start procreating, when I can guaran-*frickin'*-tee you we never had such a conversation.

"No, we didn't. I'm not ready."

"Fuck!" And then he muttered a bunch of other things under his breath.

"What was that?" I challenged.

His eyes flashed blue fire at me. "I *said*, 'Fuck, this is exactly the communication shit Justin had been talking about.'"

I put my hands on my hips. "And what communication *shit* was Justin educating you on?"

"He said not talking is relationship kryptonite."

I snorted. Leave it to Justin to make some kind of superhero reference, even when spewing marriage advice. James picked up on my brainwave, and a ghost of a smile drifted across his face.

"He's not wrong," I said. "We should have talked about this. Clearly we've been on entirely different wavelengths. You want to start a family immediately, and I want to wait and enjoy married life for a bit."

I let out a big defeated sigh and sunk back down to sitting on the lounge chair. Not even a month into this married thing, and we were already fucking up the whole talking part of it. We'd been too busy screwing like Viagra-fueled bunnies to stop and talk about our goals and priorities. He joined me on the chair, and I turned to face him. He looked positively shattered.

"I'm old as fuck, Emma," he said, letting out his own sigh.

I watched his broad shoulders slump, and I suddenly had this all-consuming urge to run my hands over his bare skin, up and down his biceps, across his muscular back and over his defined abs and chest. I reached out and rested my hand on his forearm instead. He was warm and hard beneath my fingertips.

I shook my head. "You're not old."

"I'm *forty*. By the time you want to start trying, I'll be forty-one. Then by the time the kid gets here, if we conceive right away, I'll be forty-two. I'm old as fuck!"

I swallowed. "I'm just not ready yet ... I'm sorry. I want you all to myself for a little while. I'm still enjoying work. I just got promoted to Director of Studies at the school. I ... I just want to wait a bit."

I gripped his arm pleadingly, wanting him to see my side of it, understand where I was coming from. I wasn't ready to share him with anyone, even if that person was our baby.

"You're *not* old," I said again. "Old men don't have sex like that. Old men don't dive like that. Old men don't go for fifteen kilometre runs every day. You're the youngest forty-year-old I've ever met. And aren't you the one who keeps telling me that age is just a number?"

He hadn't been looking at me. He'd been staring at my stomach, of all places. Was he mourning something that was never there? Oh God, was this our yacht trip with Justin and Kendra two years ago all over again?

We'd only been together a couple of months when we'd had a pregnancy scare, and although I'd been relieved to find out I wasn't having a baby, James, who had initially been terrified and irate, was, in the end, incredibly disappointed we wouldn't be starting a family after only two months together.

I wasn't sure how to comfort him.

"And doesn't Justin say..." I smiled, hoping to lighten the mood. "That you're only as old as the woman you *feel*? And I'm *only* twenty-nine, so..." I let my hand slide down onto his toned thigh.

The corner of his mouth tugged up, but it didn't stay there for long.

"What can I do to convince you that you're not old?" I gave his thigh a squeeze, and then let my fingers drift down toward his crotch. For the first time in nearly three weeks, it seemed that he was not sporting an erection.

His eyes slowly drifted upwards, and the look he was giving me was pure, unadulterated dominance. Dark and wicked, his winged brows pinched in a menacing scowl, while his eyes shone fiercely with lust. Holy mother of God, what the hell did he have planned? What the fuck did I just get myself into?

I licked my lips. "What can I do to get you to see my side?"

"You really want to know?" he asked, his voice a breath above a whisper.

I nodded. "I get that you're disappointed. And although I'm not pleased with your reaction, I don't want to fight on our honeymoon. So I'd like to make it up to you, quell this disappointment with something positive to look forward to."

I shifted in my seat, the look he was continuing to give me was making me a tad uneasy. It was unwavering. It was stripping. I was naked in his eyes and probably bound and plugged and with a bright red ass.

A slow smile coasted across his face, winding me. Blinding me. He smiled rarely. At least he didn't when he wasn't around me, or so I've been told. But even when he didn't smile my man had a gorgeous, sexy mouth. Talented as all get out, too. With full, but firm lips and straight white teeth. Often though, set in a stern line, giving nary a clue to his thoughts. He'd perfected the mask of indifference early on in his life. Keeping his feelings out of the equation. Not letting anyone in or any emotions out. And although he wasn't generous with the smiles, when he did he could flash the most dazzling, boyishly playful grin or a smug and confident challenging smirk at the drop of a hat. His slow smiles were evocative little teases, saying so much without hardly moving a muscle. Laying out his wicked intentions with no more than the crook of a lip. Yes, my man was an enigma. Multi-faceted and complex. A man who when he walked into a room every man wanted to be and every woman wanted to be with, and he was mine. All mine. Forever.

"I want to gag you," he said softly, the rigid lacing of his abs flexing as he sat up straight. "I want to restrain you in a thigh sling and wrist cuffs, and I want to flog your ass until it's pink and tears stream down your face. I want to hear you moan and whimper against the gag as your pussy quivers around my cock when I take you from behind."

My bottom lip dropped open, and I felt my nipples harden against my bathing suit top. Anticipation and perhaps a dollop of fear careened through my body, ending between my thighs, where my core clenched tight with curiosity and need. James had brought up gagging early on in our relationship, saying it turned him on to hear a woman moan against a gag, but I'd refused a ball or ring gag, compromising and going with just a silk scarf or a piece of leather firmly tied around my head and between my teeth. It was uncomfortable, but it didn't really hinder my breathing the way a real gag would.

"Umm ..."

"You know I'd never hurt you, right?"

"I know."

"But we're married now ... and you've become so adventurous in the last few years, I thought that maybe you'd want to take things one step further. Try the gag again."

My eyes went wide. "Do you have a ball gag *here*? On the boat?"

He nodded. "I have a few things ... a few surprises."

More surprises? Holy hell, he'd been surprising me for weeks. A new flogger, a new riding crop, a new butt plug, new anal beads, new nipple clamps—oh God, the nipple clamps! A cock ring with a vibrating clit stimulator. Good thing we'd flown private, otherwise he probably would have been pulled into security when the border guard saw what was stashed in his suitcase.

My chest heaved, and I realized I was panting. I put my hands to my cheeks. They were on fire, and it wasn't just from the blazing sun overhead. Holy mother of God, was I ever turned on. And like a male lion catching the scent of a lioness in estrus, his nostrils flared, and his eyes grew dark. He stood up from where he was sitting next to me and scooped me into his arms; I went willingly, wrapping my arms around his neck, our argument long forgotten, and the need to mate, to be one and connected the only thing passing between us.

He made his way down the first set of stairs and stopped, and then cradling me with one hand, he dug into the pocket of his shorts and brought out my birth control.

"What would you do if I tossed it overboard right now?" he asked darkly.

Well, shit, apparently this conversation *wasn't* over.

"I'd throw you the fuck overboard, too, and make you go get it," I said cheekily, meeting his gaze dead on and not blinking. He might be a successful business tycoon and have men cowering under him daily, but I wasn't a man, and I wasn't a coward. I was his wife. I was his equal.

His eyebrows shot up on his forehead.

"Don't fucking mess with me, Shaw. I'm seriously contemplating tossing your ass in the drink right now anyway. That bit of bravado up there was not cool. Stomping upstairs like some big he-man, demanding to know why I was taking birth control. I thought we were past all this. I thought we were headed downstairs to our room so you could gag me and flog me."

Okay, now I was pissed. We were finally in a good place again, and he had to go and ask a stupid question like that. What the hell was wrong with him?

He growled low in his throat and then put me down onto my feet.

"I'm still not happy about this, Emma. I don't want to wait. I know you want to, but I hate that you have all the control here."

Aha! Finally, we were at the root of it. Mr. Control Freak didn't like that he wasn't the one calling the shots, that he wasn't the one dictating when we started a family. For the most part in our relationship, I let James take the lead. He was an alpha male by nature and a bossy fucker, used to getting his way. And I'm pretty easygoing, all things considered. I take everything day by day and go with the flow. But if something he did or decided didn't sit right with me, I spoke up. I'd allowed a man to run roughshod over my life for nearly nine years, so I had no intention of letting it happen again. And James knew that when I did voice my opinion, he needed to listen and consider it. We'd had our fair share of rip-roaring fights early on where I set the boundaries and expectations for our relationship. I wasn't going to be stepped on and ignored, and he knew that now.

I rolled my eyes at him, tossed the packet of birth control onto a nearby table, along with my sunglasses and sarong, and then I walked to the back of the boat. "I don't know about you, Shaw, but I need to cool off." And then, with a sly smile over my shoulder, I dove like a graceful mermaid into the briny deep.

"**O**h God, I needed that!" I said, giggling as we both climbed up the ladder on the back of the boat, having swum around and frolicked like porpoises in the refreshing and crystal-clear water. We were anchored in a bay just off Rangiroa in the Tuamotu islands, and although the beach in front of a beautiful resort was loaded with people and several other boats were anchored around us, we were still all alone, and the freedom of that solitude was welcoming.

"Yeah," he said. "Me too."

He grabbed two towels off a bench and handed me one, running his hands up and down my arms to help dry me off.

I blinked up at him, water dripping down my face while the sun warmed my skin. "Let's go downstairs. You can take control there. Because I'm sorry, bub, but I'm not budging on this. I'm just not ready."

His lips pursed in thought for a second and then he nodded, running the towel over his head and then slinging it around his neck. "Fine. You relinquish your body to me today ... and for the rest of the trip, and I won't bring up the baby thing again."

I felt the butterflies in my belly begin to taxi down the runway.

"But ..." His mouth turned up into a wry smile. "That doesn't mean that once we're back in Canada, I'm not going to bring the issue up again. Maybe you go off the pill and we not actively try, but just see what happens?"

I let out an exasperated sigh through my nose and then hung the towel on a rack so it could dry.

"You're annoying sometimes, you know that? Incessant and relentless."

And then suddenly I found myself scooped back up into his arms, and he was carrying me down to our bedroom.

"Oh, but baby, most of the time you love how relentless I am, especially when my head is between your legs."

I rolled my eyes but nodded. He had me there.

CHAPTER 8

"Just like that, princess, don't move. Oh fuck, you look so damn sexy, all trussed up with nowhere to go." He had me practically hogtied. Okay, hogtied is a garish description, but I certainly *felt* hogtied. Plus, I'd actually vetoed the hogtie position when he'd suggested it. We'd tried it before, it was uncomfortable as hell, and I'd hated it.

I was on the bed, on my knees, with straps around my thighs and cuffs around my wrists. The cuffs were attached to the thigh straps so I couldn't lift my arms at all. I was in the presentation position, not that we ever acknowledged it, but if we did, that was the position I was in. On my knees, hands on my thighs and open for inspection. And by the way he was ogling me, his eyes raking my body from top to bottom and back again, filled with lust and desire, I knew he liked what he saw.

I was completely naked, my hair was wet and clinging to my skin all down my back, and I trembled like a leaf in a windstorm—part nerves but mostly aroused, incredibly aroused. I felt a small trickle of said arousal drip its way down my inner thigh as I knelt on the bed in front of him—waiting.

I knew what was coming next—the gag! Only I had no idea what *kind* of gag. Was he going to use a ring, so I could still breathe normally? It'd just be uncomfortable, and I'd wind up drooling like a basset hound. Or was he going to go straight for the ball gag, compromise my breathing so he could hear me moan?

"Now ..." His voice sent a frisson of need coursing through my body. "I'm going to gag you as well, okay, baby?"

"Do I have a choice?" I muttered.

Smack.

I yelped and shifted slightly on the bed. He'd fucking flogged me! The bastard had just flogged my ass. I hadn't even seen it in his hands. Where had he been hiding it?

"You *always* have a choice." His voice was low and dark and so sexy I felt my nipples grow hard and watched them turn a dark crimson. "But that little bit of sass earned your fine ass a spank. Now, again, I'm going to gag you, okay?"

I bit my lip to hide my smile. He was so easy to rile; it wasn't even funny. "Okay."

"Good!"

Another *whack* of the flog to the left cheek had me moaning and squirming where I knelt. That swift bite of pain, followed by a blossoming heat that spread across my skin in a sublime warmth, was like a gloriously sexy hug. If I could, I'd wrap my arms around such a feeling and never let go. Only I couldn't wrap my arms around a damn thing; the man had made sure of that.

"Now, back to the gag ..." He knelt up on the bed and came toward me. "I'm going to use a ball gag on you. I have a ring, in case you don't like the ball, but I would like to try the ball first. I think you'll actually like it. I want to hear your restrained moans and groans as I flog your ass and then fuck your pussy. Maybe later I'll fuck your ass."

Oh God, yes, please!

I swallowed. My eyes went wide as he pulled the gag out from behind him, a big red silicone ball between the two leather straps.

"Open up, princess." He wrapped the strap around my head and placed the ball in my mouth. It wasn't enormous—I'd had jawbreakers bigger than this when I was a kid—but it certainly wasn't a gumball, either. I fixed it behind my teeth and bit down. It squished slightly but then pushed back, and I felt a slight twinge in my jaw. I was going to feel this later.

He tightened the strap around my head and pulled, making sure it was good and snug.

"How's that feel?"

I blinked up at him and nodded. It didn't feel great, but it wasn't painful either, just weird and uncomfortable was all. So far, though, I wasn't sold on the whole *gag* thing, but I'd agreed to do this for James. I was busting out my feminine wiles and making all kinds of kinky promises to take his mind off the fact that I wasn't ready to have kids yet. And really, I'm sure I'd be having an orgasm or two, so the price was worth it, in my opinion.

Once he made sure the gag was tight enough and it wouldn't slip out from between my lips from his rhythmic pounding, he pulled a chain from his pocket to reveal the nipple clamps.

YES!

Making sure they were good and tight, he clipped them on to my aching peaks, being sure to suck them into his mouth first. Fierce pulls of suction and little nips had them forming rigid points and all the blood rushed to the surface, making them good and hard and so sensitive.

He gave the chain connecting the crocodile-toothed clamps a swift tug, and I gasped from the intense burst of pain. "You're mean," I tried to say, but the gag inhibited my speech, and all that came out was a garbled mess.

His smile stole the breath in my chest. "You love it." He got up off the bed and stalked around to the side of me. "Are you nervous?" He asked, his shorts obscenely tight from his raging erection. He followed my gaze and grinned, and then slowly, almost like he was doing a bit of a strip tease, he pulled his shorts down. His beautiful cock sprang free, its silky purple head glowing with that delicious bead of pre-ejaculate and staring me down with its one eye.

I swallowed and shook my head. No, not nervous. Excited, perhaps a bit worried about how my jaw was going to feel tomorrow, but nervous? No. I trusted James implicitly, and I knew he'd never hurt me or push me too far; he knew my limits and respected them.

I saw his arm move out of the corner of my eye, and then the resounding *smack* of the flog against the back of my thigh made me flinch. Two more, rapid-fire speed and hard as hell, came at me, one more on the back of the other thigh, and the last one on my upper back. That one stung like a bitch.

"Hmmm." I heard him hum behind me. "I think I might blindfold you for this, too. At least for a little while, so I really have the element of surprise. You'll never know what's coming next." I watched him walk over to the big dresser where we'd unloaded our suitcases, and he opened a drawer. He brought out a dark black sash and then knelt back up onto the bed. Our eyes locked, hazel to soul-penetrating blue. "I love you, Emma," he said. And then he brought the sash up over my eyes and tied it behind my head.

I swallowed the sudden hard lump that had formed in my throat as my bright and beautiful world suddenly went dark and he gently tied the soft fabric behind me. I was struck dumb by his confession, especially at such an odd time, when I was bound and gagged and preparing to be his sex slave. But leave it to James to pull the rug out from under me. Even when he was getting ready to flog my ass, he still showed me how much he loved me, how much he cared.

A finger lightly traced the curve of my jaw, and I instinctively turned into his touch, closing my eyes at how much I loved the feeling of his skin against mine. No matter how or where, I craved his touch. I moaned as he tugged on the nipple clamp again, sending the ache and need straight through my body to my clit, while another drop of arousal landed on the sheet below me.

I felt his weight shift on the bed, and then his hands came up under my arms, and he guided me down to the mattress so that I was lying on my back. He helped me bend my legs and put my arms down by my sides. It wasn't nearly as uncomfortable as the hogtie; this was actually quite pleasant.

Once he made sure I was in the proper position, he dragged my body down to the foot of the bed so that my toes hung over and my butt was right on the edge. A long, lone finger swept up through my folds, and then I heard him moan, followed by the quick *pop* of him removing his finger from his mouth.

"Mmm, so sweet, and all mine."

That was one thing that had always thrown me for a bit of a loop with my husband, from early on in our relationship. He was a talker when we were getting busy. More often than not it was dirty talk, filthy talk, downright nasty talk, and I freaking love it. But sometimes, when he was buried balls-deep inside me, taking my body to places no man has ever taken it, that's when he poured his heart out, tore down his walls and showed his vulnerable side.

It was always a little jarring as I was ready to get busy and get my rocks off, tear each other's clothes off and claw up his back like a starved wolverine, and yet there he was, telling me he needed me more than he needed air and that I'd saved him. Sometimes, I hated to admit it, I'd tell him to shut up, quit the jabbering and fuck me silly, because as much as I loved to see his sensitive side, it could be a bit of a mood-killer.

So a part of me was worried that he was going to go there again, get all sensitive and sweet on me, while I was gagged, blindfolded and bound like prize-winning heifer.

"You won't stay in this position long, baby. It's not safe with the gag. You might choke on your saliva. But I just want you here for a couple minutes so I can spank your sweet little pussy properly." And then, without further ado, I heard the familiar whistle through the air, and then the flog came down over top of my mound and pussy lips with a *fwack*.

I moaned against the gag in my mouth and writhed on the bed as the intense pain brought every nerve ending in my body alive and on end, while a beautiful heat slowly took the place of the sting and started to spread across my skin. The pain was intense, but so was the pleasure. Another, and another, to the inside of each thigh, and then one more to the top of my mound and lips. With each flog, I moaned and groaned and strained against my restraints, tugged on the straps and let my head thrash from side to side. And again, and again, and again, right across my most sensitive flesh, he brought down the tassels, until I lost count and each one seemed to blend into the next and my clit throbbed and my folds swelled and ached for more. I ground my pelvis up into the air, desperate for friction but getting none. All the while, James just continued with the torment.

I could feel the saliva building in my mouth and pooling at the back of my throat. I swallowed a couple of times, but things were starting to feel uncomfortable and a little alarming. If he made me go much longer in this position, I was going to have to ask him stop.

As if reading my mind, he helped me sit up, but not before tugging hard and firmly on the nipple clamps and making me mewl against the gag as the jolt of pain soared through my body and hit my clit like a battering ram. He hadn't even touched me with his tongue yet, and already I was a damp and panting mess, saturated with need and ready to combust on the spot, and all from the glorious flogging!

He helped me up and turned me around, guiding my body and limbs because I couldn't see anything. I was starting to enter that loopy headspace a lot of submissives get into when they've been tortured to the point of pure exhaustion and near mind-loss from all the pleasure.

He tucked a pillow under my chest and cheek so that I wasn't just face-down on the bed, and I tilted my head to one side, the gag strap pressing into my face just a touch while the ball shifted slightly and the left side of my jaw was able to relax a bit. My wrists were still bound to my thighs, so I wasn't really on all fours. I was more on all two, up on my knees, with my legs spread slightly, my face on the pillow and my arms just hanging there. But, as weird as the position may sound, and as awkward as I'm sure it may have looked, it was actually rather comfortable. I swallowed the saliva that had backed up in my throat again, and this time it wasn't nearly as difficult and didn't set off any alarm bells. We were good to go.

James wasted no time, and as soon as he made sure I was comfortable, he brought the flogger back down across my ass cheeks, only to then trail the silky soft suede up the length of my back, drawing out gooseflesh and tickling me just right. I squirmed from the different sensations. One minute I was in pain from the smack, and the next I was being tickled to within an inch of my sanity; the man was relentless and incredibly creative.

He reached beneath me and pulled on the chain of the nipple clamps again, while at the same time swirling the tassels of the flogger across my butt cheeks and down the backs of my thighs. It was pain and pleasure all at once, and my brain couldn't compute. It couldn't make heads or tails of how I was supposed to feel, and I quickly felt myself slipping off into a bit of a dream world again. The gentle rock of the boat, the heady scent of sex in the room, combined with the salt air and James' always alluring scent of man, the sensations were hypnotic and I was starting to feel a bit drunk.

And then just when I felt like I was going to drift off completely, a warm, velvety tongue swept up me from behind, starting with my clit, through my folds and then finishing with a swirl around my anus. What the hell? He'd never put his mouth on me there before.

Zipping back to reality from my subspace, I wriggled on the bed and shook my head, moaning in protest. No, he couldn't do this. No, no, no!

"Emma?" He stopped the incredible torment with his tongue, his hands kneading the cheeks on my ass with his nimble fingers. "Are you okay?"

I shook my head and made a "nuh-uh" sound.

"Are you wanting me to stop licking your ass?"

I nodded.

"Is it because you don't like it? Or because you think it's wrong and dirty?"

Wrong and dirty! It didn't hurt. It felt amazing. But it was so wrong. Wasn't it? We did a lot of filthy shit. A LOT! But never this. This just felt like a whole new level of filth. Could we go there?

"Is it painful?" he asked again, his voice suddenly filled with concern.

I shook my head.

"Does it feel good?"

I hesitated before I nodded. He'd know if I were lying. Mewling, I shifted on the bed beneath his palms and against the restraints. It was mind-blowing, but it was also so wrong.

"So you just want me to stop because you think it's wrong?"

I nodded again, but this time it was with far less conviction.

He chuckled low and menacing in this throat. "Ah, well, I'm sorry, my love, but that's not a good enough reason for me to stop. You're my wife, and if I'm cool licking your ass until you shatter into a million beautiful little pieces in front of me, then I'm going to do it. There is nothing wrong with making your wife come until she passes out. And besides, you know I'm a dirty bugger."

One finger rimmed my tight hole, and I clenched, my body betraying my brain as it so often did when it came to James and his wicked and dirty ideas.

"If you honestly want me to stop, Emma, I will. Do you want me to stop?" That finger was awfully curious, making its way between my cleft, only to draw more wetness back up between my cheeks and make decadent little circles.

And then I felt his tongue flick my anus again and I nearly came on the spot. Finally, I shook my head. No, he could continue; God, how I wanted him to continue. With a triumphant chuckle, he dove back in with the vigor of a starved man who'd just been given a loaf of bread.

I stop myself, I just couldn't. I pushed back into his face as he lapped at my sensitive rosette, pulling my butt cheeks apart so he could swirl his magnificent tongue around and around, until I was a shaking and convulsing mess on the bed. Strangled cries fought their way past the gag but came out as nothing more than muffled groans, while saliva dripped down and around the ball and onto the bed. And then, just when I thought I was going to lose my mind, he stopped and something cold and hard pressed against me, ordering refuge. I pushed out with my muscles and gave in to the demand. It was a butt-plug of sorts, I'm sure, but based on the girth and how it stretched me until I cringed, it was one we'd never used before.

Fingers found their way to my swollen clit and began to rub evocative little circles, while the other hand continued to push the plug in further. I groaned against the gag and shook my head again. It was too big. He had to stop.

"Stop!" I tried to say, my whole body wiggling to get his attention.

"Does that hurt?" he asked.

I nodded.

"Okay." He pulled it out a little bit. My body began to relax, and my head stopped thrashing. I no longer felt as though I was going to be split in half by a silicone sex toy. "Better?"

I hummed and nodded. Much better.

His fingers continued their torment while he twisted the plug, but didn't push it in any further. I was all for pain and pleasure, but that was just downright agony. And then I felt it, his cock, hard and eager, pressing against my pussy lips. I pushed myself back into him again and spread my legs, welcoming him home.

Slowly, ever so slowly, torturously so, he sank himself inside me, inch by luscious inch, until I was begging against the gag for him to go harder, go faster, to just fuck me stupid.

Once I knew he was in, I pushed back into him again and squeezed my muscles around him. He stopped twisting the plug but didn't remove his fingers from my clit. Using his one free hand, he gripped my hip and started to move.

My body was a swirling vortex of erotic sensations. Pain and pleasure melded together until I couldn't discern one from the other and every smack, every tug, every flog just felt divine. The nipple clamps, the plug, his fingers, his cock, and even the gag in my mouth and the fact that I was forced to breathe through my nose was kind of starting to turn me on. I was full. Consumed. Claimed. The man had taken care of everything, filled me to the brim and made sure no major erogenous zone was being ignored. Moaning against the gag, I continued to take everything he had to give me, thrusting my ass into his pounding pelvis while his fingers dug deep into my hip and his cock punished my pussy.

He took my clit between his thumb and forefinger and began to tug, rubbing it between the two until it was hard and engorged. The orgasm knocked at the door; hell, it pounded on it. Screaming to be let free—to be unleashed.

"You're close, baby, I can tell. So close. Your pussy is so wet, so greedy."

I mewled against the gag and shoved myself further onto his shaft, desperate to feel him hit the end of me, my body gripping him like a fist, unwilling to let go of him until I got my release. I was going to black out soon if I didn't come, I could feel it. My brain was starting to get cloudy again; saliva dribbled from my lips, and my pussy continued to trickle down between my thighs.

"Come for me, Emma." His voice low and commanding. His rhythm started to wane as his climax drew close, and then as a final plea for me to join him on the leap off the cliff, he pulled down and pinched my clit hard, picked up the speed of his thrusts, gripped my hip tight and let go. His snarl was wild and feral as he poured himself inside me, his cock pulsing against my walls, while his fingers picked up their erotic circles.

I clenched around him again, pushed into him and jumped off the cliff. Down, down, down I spiralled off the mountaintop. Bright, beautiful lights flashed behind my closed eyelids, while my entire body thrummed alive and on fire as the orgasm tore through me from tip to tail and back again, swirling around my belly and out through my limbs. I groaned against the ball gag, and then suddenly I felt James' hand release my hip, and he began fumbling behind my head. The gag loosened and tumbled out of my mouth, and then the sash around my eyes was pulled free. I blinked at the sudden glaring light flooding in from the big bedroom windows.

My chest heaved against the pillow as my breaths came out in ragged gasps, while sweat misted my skin. I worked my jaw back and forth slowly, feeling the dull ache from having kept it open for so long. Yep, I'd definitely be feeling that one tomorrow. James slipped himself and the plug from me and then went to task releasing me from my bonds; big hands massaged my wrists and where the strap had wrapped around my thighs, working the circulation back into the joints and skin.

Once I found a decent headspace again and was able to put one thought in front of the other, and then eventually one foot in front of the other, I toddled off to the washroom to pee. I joined James in the bedroom a few minutes later, and he handed me a glass of water. I chugged it greedily, not caring two hoots that it trickled down my chin and bare chest in rivulets; I was so thirsty.

He led me over to the bed, where we sat on the edge, and drawing the blanket that was draped across the end, he unfolded it and wrapped it around my shoulders before picking me up and plunking me in his lap.

"So ..."

I let my lids flutter shut and leaned into him, my head against his chest. "That was fun."

"It was, wasn't it?"

"Mhmm."

"What did you think of the gag?"

I worked my jaw back and forth a couple times before answering. "It was uncomfortable. I'm not going to lie. But at the same time, once you were inside me, the plug was in my ass and the gag in my mouth, I was pretty turned on. I felt very full. And the fact that I had to only breathe through my nose, I think that heightened things a little too. It made my head kind of loopy."

"Well, I fucking loved hearing you moan against it. See, feel ... I'm getting hard again just thinking about it."

I shook my head with a light snort and wriggled in his lap. "Can I see that butt-plug? It was massive." He tilted his head at the dresser, where lo and behold *Big Bertha,* or so she should be named, lay thick, pink and foreboding, staring me down. I squinted at Bertha. "Is that a suction cup on the bottom?"

He nodded. "Yeah. One day, I'd like to stick it to the wall of the shower, or a glass surface or something, have you slide onto it and then fuck you." My mouth dropped open, and I stared at him. But he just grinned. "One day. That day doesn't have to be today. It's big. We'll work you up to it."

I swallowed and nodded. "Yeah, it's big."

Chuckling, he pulled me tighter against him. "Shall we nap, baby? You seem drained."

I yawned and then stretched my arms against him before sliding off his lap and slithering my way up toward the pillows. "Yeah, let's nap. And then when we wake up, you can try that *Big Bertha* beast again. Might as well start working me up to it today."

His eyes flashed blue lightening as he stalked toward me on the bed. "You are seriously the best wife ever." He snuggled down behind me, and we nestled into the spoon position.

I linked my fingers with his and closed my eyes. "Well, I certainly try."

CHAPTER 9

A few days later, I was rummaging around in my nightstand drawer looking for my birth control pills, as James had woken me up at the crack of dawn with a big, demanding rod in my back, so I'd forgotten to take it when I woke up. He'd fucked me good and then scooped me up and carried me off to the shower, only to fuck me *great* again in there, until I was putty covered in soap bubbles and so sated I needed a nap.

I tore the drawer apart looking for the pills but came up empty. Then I checked behind the nightstand, behind the bed, under the bed, in every dresser drawer, my suitcase, my toiletries bag, the medicine cabinet in the bathroom, even the drawer of debauchery as I'd nicknamed it, where James kept all our kinky things, and I couldn't find them. I'd taken my pill the day before when I woke up, and I couldn't remember putting it anywhere new, so where on earth could it have gone?

I wandered out to the back of the boat where James was busy fishing. An avid fisherman back home, he took every opportunity he had to cast a line out into the crystal-clear water with the hopes of catching a trophy for dinner. So far he'd been pretty successful, having landed a beautiful mahi mahi, and then a few days later a delicious marlin. It helped that Ezra, one of the deckhands we'd employed, was also a fishing guide and knew all the best places to take James so he could attempt to "land the big one."

"Hey, babe?"

He had just placed his rod in the holder, so I knew his attention was no longer otherwise occupied. I rested my hand on his back, feeling his hard, toned muscles flex beneath my palm. He was warm, and the sun was bronzing his skin so beautifully, he reminded me of a statue, standing tall and fierce in a town square, protecting all who lived there.

He spun around to face me with a big grin, his sunglasses masking those beautiful blue eyes. "Yeah, princess, what's up?"

"Have you seen my birth control? I've looked everywhere, and I can't find the little pack. I took it yesterday, but today it's gone."

He didn't move. I wasn't even sure he was breathing anymore. And then I saw his throat undulate, and a muscle along his chiseled and scruffy jaw twitched just ever so slightly.

"Have you seen my birth control?"

He swallowed. "Yes."

I let out a grateful sigh. "Oh good, where?"

He swallowed again. "I, uh ... I tossed them into the water."

I wasn't sure what came over me. No, wait, I'm entirely sure what came over me. It was pure unadulterated white-hot rage, and with strength and power I didn't even know I had, I reared back, placed two hands in the center of his chest and pushed him overboard.

I'm not stupid. Or maybe I am. I'd gone and pledged my life to a deceitful, control-freak moron with eyes of sapphire and hair of coal. But either way, stupid or not, I am organized, and I am a planner. Prepared for everything, even that which you can't prepare for. So even though I was on the pill, and we'd stopped using condoms just a few months into our relationship, I'd packed some rubbers anyway, just in case. In case of what? I don't know, but I'd tossed a twenty-four pack of magnum extra-thins into my suitcase as I was packing a few weeks ago. So if James hadn't already been eaten by sharks or barracuda, and if I ever forgave him, he'd be wrapping up that sperm-shooting shaft of his until we got back to Canada and I could get another prescription.

Livid, I took to the small onboard gym and started to run on the treadmill. Exercise almost always helped clear my head, and right now my brain was so full of fire I was a tad surprised that when I watched myself get sweaty and red-faced in the big floor-to-ceiling mirror, steam didn't also start to shoot from my ears.

How could he do that? We'd discussed things. We'd come to an understanding. I'd promised kinky and wicked things in exchange for him waiting until the spring to start a family. I wasn't ready. And yet it seemed to have gone in one ear and out the other. And rather than respect my choice and my body, he'd decided to get manipulative and sneaky and withhold my choice from me.

We'd vowed early on in our relationship to never use sex as a weapon. I would never deny him sex as a way to get back at him for something, never hold it over his head or threaten no sex unless I got my way. But it would seem that my dear, sweet husband had decided to play by his own set of rules, so I guess I could as well. And at that moment, I wasn't sure I'd ever let his cock get near me again.

I'm not sure how long I ran. Maybe twenty minutes, maybe an hour. But by the time I turned off the treadmill, I was soaked to the bone in sweat, and my face rivaled a beet. Mopping up my forehead with a big, white towel, I didn't see him enter the gym. I didn't even smell him, probably because his impromptu swim had washed away his manly scent.

I wrapped the towel around my neck and glared at him. He cowered under my stare and, like a scolded dog, averted his eyes, instead fixing them on my feet.

"I can't believe you!"

He rolled his bottom lip between his teeth before bringing his eyes up to meet mine again. It'd been a while since I'd seen him look this sheepish, this guilty.

"So what, you just thought I'd forget completely to stop taking my pills? Pills I've taken every day for the last ... I don't know, like thirteen years? Do you think I'm that *stupid*?"

His eyes went wide, and he shook his head stiffly. "No, you're not stupid."

I ground my back teeth together. "Well, obviously you must think I am if you assumed I wouldn't notice my pills were missing."

"I ... Emma." And then he reached into his pocket and pulled something out. "Here." I snatched it from him. It was my birth control. What the actual fuck was going on?

I closed my eyes and shook my head. I needed to get off this boat. I needed to set foot on dry land, see other people, smell something besides the sea; I needed space. Pushing past him, I set out to find Ezra.

"Hi!" I said with far more enthusiasm than I felt in my heart.

Ezra nodded with a big, genuine smile, his brown eyes dancing as he tidied up a few things with the dive equipment. "Hello, Mrs. Shaw. How are you?"

"Getting a little seasick, actually. And I've told you a million times, Ezra, call me Emma."

It was hard to tell given how dark brown his skin was, but I'm pretty sure he was blushing. "Yes, Miss Emma."

I rolled my eyes and grinned at him. "That's better, I guess. Would you mind taking the boat into land, wherever the closest port is. I'd love to get out and explore for a bit. As much as I love being out here, I fear all I have are sea legs now and, well, I'm getting a little sick of them."

His mouth stretched into a wide and knowing smile. He'd been within earshot when I'd confronted James about the pills, and the splash my husband's big body had made in the water could be heard over the entire boat.

He nodded again. "Sure thing, ma'am. We're not too far from Huahine. We can be there in a couple hours and dock for the night, if that works for you?"

I smiled at him. "That sounds perfect. Thank you, Ezra."

I locked myself in our bedroom for the remainder of the day. I read, I slept, I read some more. I caught up on emails, checked in on things at work and even Skyped Alyssa to tell her how big of a dink my husband was being. She'd agreed and said I should have shoved chum in his pockets before I tossed him overboard. Would have made him an easier target for the sharks to find.

James hadn't even tried to talk to me. I heard him shuffle past the locked bedroom door a couple of times. Watched as his big shadow stopped for a moment or two, but he never knocked, never said anything, and then eventually he'd walk away, only to return a while later and repeat.

Although Alyssa had made light of the situation and suggested I turn my husband into bait, she'd also brought up the fact that although my aggravation was founded, the true topic of our argument was kind of dumb. This man loved me more than anything in the world, and he wanted to have a family with me. That was the root of all of it. But the branches of it were what bothered me, the lies and the deception, the blatant thievery and the fact that he just expected me to not notice that a part of my everyday routine was missing. That he was trying to control my body and my choices to fit his needs.

It was roughly three-thirty when we docked in Huahine. Ezra came down and rapped on my door to let me know the boat had been moored and we were all set to go about and explore. Only when James met me on the top deck, I ignored him completely and walked off down the dock.

"Emma!" he called. "Emma, come on! Princess!" His big, sandaled feet made a thunderous *clomp, clomp* on the wooden dock as he loped after me. "Come on, baby, I'm sorry."

I spun around to face him. "You know, that's the first apology I've heard. So far you've said very little and instead tried to subdue me with puppy-dog eyes, silence and space."

His face fell.

"I need some space. I need some time away from you, away from us.

We've been locked on that boat for weeks, and when we do go into town, it's always together. I need a break."

He reached for me. "I said I was sorry."

I pulled away from his grasp. "And I said I wanted space. Give me that, and maybe I'll consider forgiving you." A new light flashed in his eyes. "I said *maybe*. I am so pissed off at you right now, James Shaw, a part of me wishes you'd been eaten by sharks." And then I spun on my flip-flops and took off down the dock, flowy skirts and mermaid tendrils getting caught up in a sudden warm gust of wind and swishing around me like a gauzy veil.

I wandered around for a little while, enjoying the sights and sounds of yet another tropical paradise. Huahine, which is part of the Society Islands, is made up of two islands, but the islands are only separated by a few hundred yards of water, so in essence, it's really just one big island.

Having done some quick research on the port when Ezra mentioned that this was where we were going to stop, I quickly realized that Huahine actually had a fairly big (not Walmart big, obviously) grocery store, and I went and stocked up on meats and cheeses, fruits and veggies and a couple of other odds and sods that we hadn't been able to find at some of the other smaller islands we'd stopped at. I'd texted Ezra to meet me at the entrance to the dock (so I wouldn't have to go back to the boat and see my husband), and he came and grabbed all the perishables.

And as I continued to wander, sipping on a delightful iced tea and munching on a chocolate bar, I heard other tourists talking about a sacred bridge and eels. So I politely interrupted and asked what they were talking about.

"There's a bridge, not too far from here," a gentleman of around seventy started to explain. He had a soft English accent and a mop of curly white hair that fell over his tanned and creased forehead in delightful little ringlets. "It crosses over a stream, and in the stream are these enormous eels. Over a meter long. You can buy mackerel and feed them."

"Oh, cool. Is it far?"

His friend, a woman of similar age and with a giant peach sunhat and turquoise moo-moo style dress, shook her head. "No, not too far. We've rented a car for the day if you'd like to join us. We're heading there now."

I smiled at them. "I'd love to."

And then Rupert and his best friend since kindergarten, Millie, and I piled into their rented car and took off to go see some eels.

By the time I got back to the boat, it was dark, and I was in a far better mood than when I'd left. Turned out Rupert and Millie were on a boat themselves. Members of a yacht club out of Wales, they and eight others were on a two-week sailing trip around the Society Islands. But their fellow passengers were all trapped on board with food poisoning, something about undercooked pork, while Rupert and Millie, who liked to boast that their vegetarian lifestyle had kept them healthy as the horses they both rode as children at boarding school, took off to explore Huahine on their own.

The three of us had a wonderful time at the sacred bridge visiting the blue-eyed eels. We watched as local children stood on the edge of the stream, their feet a few inches deep in the water, while the eels swam right up and around their ankles as they dropped canned mackerel into their mouths.

After the eels, Rupert and Millie treated me to dinner at the yacht club restaurant, where the three of us dined like royalty, me on fresh crab and they on a series of exotic root vegetables, fruits and legumes. The two kept me in stitches the entire time, regaling me with their many adventures. Turns out they both used to be in the cruise ship industry and had traveled the globe. But having grown up in the 1950s and '60s with prim and proper English parents—I think Rupert said his father was a lord or something—neither of them was allowed to express their sexuality or reveal the fact that they were gay. So instead, they married one another to stop their families from harping on them, believing to their very cores that they were soulmates but just not meant to mate. Millie claimed she was barren to dismiss any questions of children, and the two proceeded to live happily together as best friends while having successful relationships with various partners over the years.

"So what's got you moping around this beautiful treasure trove all by yourself there, sweetums?" Rupert asked, pouring himself more wine and then topping up Millie as well when she asked. He looked like the epitome of a baby-boomer cruiser, complete with the blue and white Hawaiian print shirt, the chinos and the Birkenstocks. The man even had a fanny pack and a Panama hat.

I drained my wine glass and then held it up for him as well. My husband had gone and rid the boat of all the booze, and damn if I didn't need a drink—or four. "Well, I just got married."

"Congratulations!" they both cheered, lifting their wine in a toast.

I rolled my eyes. "Thanks. Anyway, I just got married. And we're on a six-week honeymoon sailing trip through the islands. And my husband, who, I should mention, is twelve years older than me, wants to start a family now. Like right now. Like yesterday."

Millie started to nod. "But you're not ready?"

"Exactly." I nodded back. "I'm not ready. I'd like to enjoy being married for a bit. I just got a promotion at work. I'd like to wait a few months before I'm forced to share my body and my husband. Is that selfish?"

Rupert made a sound that was somewhere between a scoff and a raspberry. "Oh, honey, you are asking the wrong people. We are the epitome of selfish. Had we not been so selfish, we would have married people we didn't like, had babies we didn't want and then lived the rest of our lives miserable and sneaking off in the middle of the night to go and screw our mistresses, or in my case, misters."

Millie shook her head. "You are not selfish." Then she shot her BFF a look. "And neither are we." She turned back to face me. "You want to have kids with him someday, right?"

"Absolutely! Just not yet. I don't want to wait forever. But at least a few months before we start trying."

"So what'd he do?" Rupert dipped his finger into the leftover sauce on his plate and brought it to his mouth. His eyes closed, and he made a little humming sound as he enjoyed the last drop of his meal.

"He wigged out on me. Then we talked, and I thought everything was good. And then a few days later, I go looking for my birth control, and he's up and stolen it."

Millie's eyes went wide. "I hope you pushed the bugger overboard."

I burst out laughing. "That's exactly what I did!"

"Good!" they both said.

"We're really not the right people to ask," Millie added. "But it seems to me that your husband is just so madly in love with you, he can't wait to start a family with you and express that love even more."

Rupert craned his neck to the side and gave Millie a surprised eyebrow lift. "Listen to you getting all mushy and spewing nonsense like Dr. Phil."

Millie lifted one pudgy shoulder. "I have my moments. I blame the wine."

"But I'm just so angry with him and his deceit. He's such a control freak, and he's having a hard time coming to terms with the fact that he's not in control here. I am ... well, and Mother Nature. It's my body, and I'll knock it up when I'm good and ready."

Rupert nodded emphatically. "Here, here! To getting knocked up when we're good and ready!" And then he clinked his glass with mine again before he signalled to the waitress for another bottle to be sent over.

Although they never really helped me *solve* my husband problem, Rupert and Millie certainly helped me forget it for a while. So by the time I staggered my way down the dock and to the boat, I was far less mad at my dumb lying husband and more just shit-faced and praying I wasn't going to be too hung over the next day.

"Where have you been?" His voice was calm, flat and frightening as he sat at the back of the boat, hidden in the shadows. I slung one bare foot over the side, my flip-flops in my hand while I used the other hand to stabilize myself on the boat. It wasn't rocking, but I certainly was.

Once I found my footing, I stood up to my full height. "I was out."

"Where?"

"With friends."

"What friends?"

I rolled my eyes. "I met a couple of other tourists, Rupert and Millie from Wales, and the three of us went in their rented car to go see the eels, and then we had dinner."

"I've been worried about you."

"Yeah? Worried that I might go find a local lawyer and get him to draw up some divorce papers?"

I heard him inhale quickly, followed by a barely discernible growl. I couldn't really see his face, but I knew the man well enough to know that a thick vein probably pulsed along his corded neck, while a muscle in his strong jaw most likely ticked as he clenched and ground his molars. Meanwhile, his eyes were probably a fearsome cobalt with flashes of white flames swirling around like a storm and fixed on me in an unwavering stare. I was kind of glad I couldn't see him very well.

"No," he finally said. "You are my wife, and you've been gone for hours, and ..." He paused. "You're drunk."

"Yeah, so what? Someone made this a dry cruise, and I needed a drink. Rupert bought dinner and kept ordering more wine. Who was I to say no?"

"Who the fuck is Rupert?" He was a thread away from snapping. I could tell by the change in his tone. He was a jealous man by nature, and although over the years he'd learned to curb such green-eyed inclinations, once in a while they popped up. And tonight was one of those nights.

Just then we heard a *stomp, stomping* down the dock, followed by a fit of giggles. And then suddenly my adventure companions emerged.

"Darling, we caught you, wonderful." Rupert grinned, his arm linked through Millie's while the two of them teetered where they stood. "We wanted to give you our contact information. In case you're ever in the U.K., look us up. And we'll do the same if we're ever in Victoria. His eyes flashed up from my face to the brooding man behind me. "Well holy Queen Elizabeth the second, are you the husband?"

James made a rude noise in his throat.

Rupert turned back to me. "Honey, have his children now! If you

won't, I will. Good lord, I'd let that man stick it anywhere he wanted to."
He looked at James again and shot him a sassy smile. "Apparently an
age gap isn't a problem for you, lad, what about penis? You ever try
playing cricket for the other team?"

It was dark, but I couldn't mistake the sudden drop of James' jaw.
Meanwhile, Millie just erupted into a fit of drunken giggles.

I took a step forward and accepted the piece of paper Rupert was
handing me. They both offered me knowing winks, and Rupert gave a
big, flamboyant one to James before they spun around on their
orthopaedic heeled sandals and headed off toward their boat.

"*That* was Rupert," I said, tucking the piece of paper into my boho
shoulder bag. "Still jealous?"

Another throat sound rumbled through the air toward me.

"I'm going to bed," I said with a defeated sigh. "It might be best if
you chose another room to sleep in tonight."

Like a bloody ninja, he was up and off his perch in less than a
second, the heat from his body coming at me in waves and causing me
to sway where I stood. He gripped me by the biceps, his fingers digging
slightly uncomfortable divots into my skin.

"I will never sleep in another room than you when we are together.
Never."

Oh for fuck's sake, the he-man alpha was out. I had no patience for
this right now.

I went to wrench out of his arms, but he held on tighter. "Let me go,
James. I'm in no mood ... and no state to argue tonight. Share my bed,
don't share my bed, I don't care. But just leave me be."

He released one hand from my arm and tucked a knuckle beneath
my chin, tilting it up until I was forced to look at him, forced to gaze
into the eyes that in turn bore into my very soul, forced to stare at the
lips that drove me wild and I somehow couldn't get enough of, forced to
look at the face of the man I'd just pledged my life to for eternity. And
what I thought I'd see was a rattling bottle of rage, ready to explode, but
instead that face was shattered. Deeply devastated. A completely
shredded man.

Thick dark purple bags hung beneath those soul-piercing blue orbs, looking so lost and so sad I had to fight the urge to wrap my arms around him and comfort him. His mouth was drawn down in a sullen frown, and his bottom lip quivered ever so slightly.

His Adam's apple bobbed thick and heavy in his stubble-clad throat as he chose his words wisely. "I love you, Emma."

Despite the thousands of fermented grapes that were currently coursing through my veins, his words sobered me, and I let out a weighty sigh. "I love you too, James."

"I was stupid."

"Yes, you certainly were ... are."

The corner of his mouth twitched ever so slightly. "I can wait ... a few more months."

I fixed him with a steely glare. "Good, because I'm not budging on this." It seriously felt like déjà vu. I'd *just* said this to him a few days ago. Jesus, the man could be thick sometimes.

He swallowed again. "I can't lose you. You saved me."

I lifted my hand and ran my fingers through his soft, thick hair. It was luscious and beautiful and I loved playing with it. Tugging on the ends until he groaned, toying with the soft strands at the nape of his neck. He caught my wrist and brought my palm to his cheek, his eyes closing as he absorbed my touch. The man was mercurial. Hot-headed and on the warpath one minute and then sweet and gentle and oh so loving the next. He kissed my palm and then each finger, finishing with a bite to the pad of my thumb.

I brought my other hand up and let both drift down to rest on his shoulders. He released the death grip he had on my hip with his other hand and instead wrapped both around my back, pulling me against his body. His head fell to the crook of my neck, and he inhaled while his nose nuzzled and his hands ran the length of my back. "I can't lose you," he said again.

"You haven't lost me. And you never will. But stop being such a controlling ass. I have a say in this marriage as well. Your word is not law. No more lying. No more stealing. Otherwise, next time, I'll toss you overboard and drive away."

He pulled his head away from my neck and looked down at me. "I'm sorry for my behavior. I don't know what I was thinking."

I gave him a small smile. "You're madly in love with me and can't wait to start a family with me to express that love even more."

He opened his mouth but shut it again. "That's exactly right," he finally said, a dumbfounded look on his face.

"You can thank Millie for that bit of wisdom."

His face turned wary again as he looked down at me. "Do you forgive me? Your body, your choice. I won't steal your birth control, and we'll revisit the discussion of starting a family in the new year?"

I rose up onto my toes and kissed him before pulling back to look into his eyes. He no longer seemed like a lost puppy, but instead the contentment in my forgiveness washed over him and he looked like my James again.

"I forgive you. And yes, let's put a pin in it for now, and we'll discuss things in the new year." I nipped his jaw and felt his body respond. A low, feral growl rolled up through him while the arousal in his linen trousers prodded me in the hip.

"You're strong when you're mad," he said, dipping me low so that all I saw was a sky of endless stars and the man of my dreams above me, both breathtaking and incredibly complex. "Pushed me right off the boat."

I licked my lips and pulled him down so our lips were practically touching. "And don't you forget it. Now, take your drunk wife down to bed and *beg* for her forgiveness properly. May I suggest you use your tongue?"

His mouth stretched into a diabolical grin as he scooped me up into his arms. "I couldn't think of a better way to *beg* for forgiveness."

We were lying in bed, post-coital romp, sated and sleepy; my head was on James' chest, while his heart beat steadily beneath my ear and my fingers mindlessly played with the soft sprinkling of hair around his navel. His own fingers were dancing erotic circles around my lower back. Periodically, one would slip off course and dip down the crease of my ass.

"So ... about the whole baby thing," I started, not bothering to look up at him, not bothering to move at all. But I felt him stiffen beneath me, and his hand stilled on my back for a moment. "I'm still not willing to budge on the waiting thing, but ... I was thinking we could maybe look into getting a different kind of baby ... a *fur* baby. What do you think?"

I didn't have to see him to know he was smiling. His heart rate picked up beneath my ear, and his entire energy changed. We were so connected, so in tune to each other, that I could know whether he had a good day at work or not before he even made it through the front door.

"You want to get a dog?"

I nodded against his chest. "Yeah. I grew up with a family dog. You had Finn for years. I'd love our kids to have a pet. What do you think?"

His fingers resumed their delectable tickling. "I think that's a wonderful idea. I miss having a dog around, a foot warmer in the winter and a running buddy in the spring."

I kissed his chest and then sat up, finally turning to look at him. His eyes were bright, and the shadow that had hung over him when I'd put the kibosh on his imminent baby plans seemed to have disappeared. He was excited. This was exactly the reaction I had been hoping for. Swinging one leg over his torso, I scooted down until I was straddling his waist. He started to rise to the occasion beneath me.

"Annnnd ..." I twirled my finger around in the hair I'd been playing with earlier, "if you can wait until the new year, I'm willing to perhaps go off the pill in January, and we can see what happens. I'd still prefer to not start actively *trying* until the spring, but I'm willing to meet you in the middle on this. If we're meant to conceive sooner, then we will. How does that sound?"

Only James could look at me the way he was now and turn my insides to mush in less than a second. It was the perfect blending of fire, passion, love and pure unadulterated craving.

"That sounds like you're about to get fucked to within an inch of your sanity, Mrs. Shaw."

"Excellent," I purred, lifting up and swirling my cleft around the head of his shaft. "A fur baby now, a real baby soon. And this way the fur baby will be a year or so when the real baby arrives. They can grow up together like siblings." I sunk down and took him to the hilt, and his hands came up to grip my hips, encouraging me to pick up the pace.

James' mouth stretched into a lazy smile. The satisfaction on his face tangible. "Whatever you want, *wife*. You know I can't say 'no' to you when I'm balls-deep inside you."

I grinned. I knew this very well.

"Though all this talk of dogs has me wanting to fuck you doggy-style." And then, before I could blink, I was flipped around and tossed onto all fours, my dominating and incredibly strong husband positioning himself behind me. "Ah," he sighed, gripping my hips again and angling himself at my center, "this is more like it."

CHAPTER 10

The next day we went for another incredible dive. This time it was to a wreck, and we spent nearly an hour exploring the hundred-and-something-year-old sunken vessel and all the aquatic life that had decided to call it home. In and out of the wheelhouse and the cabin we swam, while fish of all kinds flitted up to our masks and clung to our bellies and tanks, curious about the newcomers and obviously not feeling threatened by us in the least.

Once back up on the surface, I found myself restless. It was one thing to be diving all day and then head back to dry land where a hammock, the beach, the cabin, friends and family, or even just a nice walk or kayak around the bay or island waited, but on the boat, we had none of that. When we were on our island, there was never a question of what to do next, because there was always something to do. James "The Handyman" often spent entire days fixing things or building some new outbuilding. He was never without a job or a chore, it seemed. Whereas I would spend hours wandering around the island picking fruit or collecting coconuts, tanning on the dock reading or even helping him fix whatever needed fixing.

But here, on the boat, there was nothing that needed fixing, and if it did, Ezra was on it. There was no building or contraption that needed sanding or painting, no fruit that needed picking, not even a kitchen I could cook in, because Lola took care of all the cooking here, too. So I was getting antsy, and the need for adventure and exploration was hanging over me and closing in like a thick fog.

"What you up to?" James asked, coming up behind me as I rummaged around in a drawer in the galley, searching for something, but I honestly couldn't tell you what.

I let out an exasperated sigh. "I'm bored."

He let out his own sigh while his shoulders slouched an inch or two. "Oh, thank God, so am I."

"Really?" My eyebrows shot up my forehead. "I thought you were having a great time, fishing and diving and relaxing."

He nodded. "Oh, I am. And any alone time I get to spend with you is complete heaven. And all that other stuff was great—for the first few weeks. But now I'm bored as fuck."

"Right? Me too!"

He pulled me against him and buried his face in the crook of my neck, having to bend his knees a fair bit to get down to my height. "Let's head to Bora Bora. It's only a couple hours from where we are now just off Tahaa. We'll dock, unload. Spend a week or so in a beautiful beachfront bungalow, see the island and then head home a little early. If we time it right, we can be back for Henry's first birthday."

Oh my God, that sounded incredible. I craved the feeling of buttery-soft sand between my toes, and the thought that we could rent a car and drive around the island for a few days made my whole body spark to new life. And leave it to James to want to uphold his title as world's best uncle and make it to his nephew's birthday party.

"I'll call the pilot, talk to Ezra and book us a room."

I bit my lip with excitement.

"Don't take too long. You still had more surprises for me, if I recall, and I'd love one now." My tongue ran up the length of his neck, feeling the rough bristle of his whiskers while my fingers traveled down his shorts and deftly snuck their way into the gap at the front. I started to stroke him. He flexed in my palm, vitally alive and continuing to grow hard and eager.

I dropped to my knees and fished him out, running my fingers along the silky-soft skin of him, enjoying the way his breath snagged as I tugged gently on his balls. His hand fell to my cheek and he guided my lips over his shaft, the taste of his pre-cum hitting my tongue as I let him bottom out in my throat.

I took him to the brink and beyond, reveling in his canticle of male jubilation as I swallowed everything he gave me and stroked him until his hands came under my arms and he helped me to my feet. I stood up with a satisfied smirk and licked my lips.

"Mmm. Yum."

I scarcely had a chance to blink before a growl filled my ears and my husband's lips crashed down against my mouth.

"Best. Wife. Ever," he said in between torrid kisses, his lips traveling down across my cheek and jaw to my neck, while his hands made their way from my breasts to my hips and then eventually my ass. His fingers started to draw up the back of my dress, dragging the soft fabric slowly up against my skin. I closed my eyes and let out a soft moan. The man knew how to seduce; he'd been doing it since day one.

He continued to lift the dress higher until my bikini bottoms were exposed, and then he pulled the stretchy fabric to the side and slipped two fingers inside, probing at my sensitive hole. He dipped his fingers below to find me wet and hot, and then he brought my wetness up my crease.

"I thought you had surprises for me?" I asked, inhaling quickly when one wayward finger pressed harder, demanding access. I couldn't help myself, and I pushed into his hand and welcomed his exploration.

"I do," he said gruffly, his teeth raking the edge of my jaw. "And they involve this glorious part of your body. I just want to make sure you're good and ready."

"Oh, I'm ready."

His chuckle was diabolical. "Not yet, angel. But you will be." And then, as if pinching me and waking me up from a dream, he withdrew his finger, his hand and his mouth, spun me around and gave me a hard smack on the butt. "Head downstairs. I'll be down there shortly. I expect you naked, and if you're not ... there'll be consequences." And then he took off in the opposite direction, to go and find Ezra.

I did as I was told and headed off to our room, muttering curses under my breath as I took the stairs. How dare he get me all hot and bothered only to switch gears just as I was getting ready to embrace the dark side? A cunning one, that guy was. Full of surprises and always keeping me guessing.

My body hummed with need and desire as I stripped down to my birthday suit in front of the mirror, marveling in the tan lines that made me look as though I was wearing a flesh-coloured bikini, but with nipples and areolas. I studied my body in the mirror. I've always suffered from low self-esteem. I was an ugly ducking in school and paid heavily for it with taunting and teasing. I ate lunch alone for years and never had a boy so much as call me or ask me to dance, let alone ask me out, until I was sixteen.

I was in the tenth grade when things started to change. I lost a ton of weight, started growing my hair out and had finally found a prescription that worked to get rid of the acne. To my elation, I finally drew the attention of a boy, and he soon became my very first boyfriend.

Only that boy had turned out to be a monster, and he'd used my low self-esteem and history with weight and skin issues to control me. So, even when I was okay looking, I never thought I was beautiful. Over the years, I've learned that I'm not terrible looking; in fact, I'd even go so far as to call myself pretty. I've attracted my fair share of men and even managed to snag two at once when I was backpacking through Europe. But it was James who truly opened my eyes to my own beauty, inner and outer.

The way he loved me so completely, the way he looked at me as though I were the most beautiful woman in the world, the way he constantly complimented me, took care of me, *he* made me feel beautiful. He made me feel special. He'd said before that he needed me to breathe, that I was more necessary than air, that he'd rather spend his last moments on earth kissing me than fighting for breath. And finally, for the first time in years, since meeting James, the self-esteem issues and my inner ugly duckling had started to fade.

They'd always be there somewhere, I'm sure, tucked back deep in the recesses of my subconscious, ready to waddle forward when I was having a particularly dark moment. But for the most part, James had managed to push them away. When I was with him, I felt good. I felt beautiful.

I let my hands travel down across my breasts, one slowly making its way down to the juncture of my thighs, while the other one started plucking and tweaking my pebbled nipples. I began rubbing rough and erotic circles around my already wet and swollen clit, enjoying my own touch but hoping my husband decided to join me soon, before I took care of business myself.

I closed my eyes and let my head loll back, my fingers alternating between circles and long gliding sweeps. My folds were drenched and my clit was growing hard.

The doorknob jiggled, but I didn't stop, and then there he was.

"Started without me, did you?" he asked, his voice a rough purr while his tenor was deep and thick like molasses. My belly did a somersault.

I bit my lip and snagged his gaze in the mirror. "Started, yes, but I'd love to finish together."

He was out of his shorts in seconds, another hard-on *thwacking* ready and eager against his taut belly as he ate up the distance between us in three long strides.

He sunk to the ground in front of me and batted my hand away. "Let me."

With his broad shoulders he inched my knees farther apart, wrapped his hands around my hips, grabbed both butt cheeks, and then drew my cleft to his mouth.

"Mmm," he hummed. "So wet, so sweet." And then his tongue went to work, lashing up my folds and then plunging inside me, hard and fierce. I was a bucking and panting mess, shamelessly pushing myself further onto his face until I was practically sitting on it. That same curious finger as before started to draw my wetness up my crease, and then soon he was requesting sanctuary. I allowed it, pushing out with my muscles and feeling him slip inside. Another finger quickly accompanied the other.

I let out a low moan as my body stretched to accommodate him. His cock was bigger, but it still took a moment to adjust. In and out, his fingers fucked my ass, while his tongue and lips never ceased in their mission. The man was a master multitasker, and all I had to do was keep myself upright and enjoy the pleasure.

"James ..." I whispered, my fingers weaving their way through his hair and pulling gently. "I'm so close ... so very, *very* close."

"Mmmm," he hummed again, and then he stood up, opened the dresser drawer and pulled out *Bertha*. My eyes went wide. "Do you think you're ready for more, baby?" he asked, wandering over to the granite-topped side table and making sure *Bertha's* suction cup was firmly in place. He cleared off the rest of the table and then beckoned me over. I went willingly.

"If it hurts, like seriously hurts, tell me and we'll stop, okay?"

I swallowed the small lump of fear in my throat and nodded. And then, with a curt nod, he dropped back to his knees and buried his face between my legs. I was close again in seconds, thrusting into him, while my clit screamed for release and my whole body shook from the pleasure radiating through every nerve.

He stood up, grabbed the lube from the drawer, applied a generous amount to both *Bertha* and me, and then lifted me up onto his hips, sheathing himself in one hard, solid thrust. I let out a little gasp and then a sigh from how good he felt, hitting me deep right away. He moved us over a couple of steps to the end table and then slowly started to lower me. I maneuvered my bottom until I felt the tip of the big butt plug poke my anus.

James' eyes met mine. "You ready?"

I nodded. "Yeah." And then slowly, ever so slowly, almost too slowly, he started to lower me down. I pushed out with my inner muscles, breathing in and out, trying to relax my body as best I could. It was going to be a struggle, James and the big piece of silicone fighting for space in my body, but I could do it. I wanted to do it.

"You're doing great, baby. Holy fuck, I feel it. Oh ... God."

I continued to breathe deeply, slowly feeling as though I was being torn in two, filled to the absolute brim. It was a big piece of equipment. The base was enormous, thicker than James for sure, and the further I sunk down, the more it started to burn. James' hand shifted on my butt, and he gripped the base of the plug.

"You can do it, baby. Just one more inch. You're so close."

I pushed out more with my muscles, closed my eyes, took a deep breath and dropped that last inch.

James snarled in my ear. "Holy fuck! This is so fucking hot!"

"Oh, God."

He started to move, bucking into me with slow measured thrusts while his fingers kneaded my butt cheeks and his cock pumped inside me, coaxing my release forward, and it was coming at him hard and fast. I felt full. So very, very full. James' big beautiful cock filled my pussy, hitting my G-spot and demanding I come, while the thick plug in my ass hit erogenous zones only the depraved are daring enough to uncover. His pelvic bone grazed my clit just enough to make my eyes roll back into my head, and within seconds, I was screaming, clawing up his back and biting his shoulder to muffle my strident cries.

"Look at me!" he commanded.

My head snapped up and our eyes locked. I swallowed hard from his dark and dangerous look and then James lunged forward and smashed his mouth against mine. I knew I'd have bruises and a fat lip later, but I didn't care. I met his ferocity with my own and thrust my tongue into his mouth, twirling and twisting and exploring.

Whimpering against his lips I let him take the lead, the orgasm was tearing through me like a machete in a hayfield, shredding and decimating everything and anything in its path, until I was left limp and boneless, forced to pull away from his torrid kisses and collapse against his chest and fighting to open my eyes. Seconds later, James found his release, and he stilled, spilling himself inside while continuing to squeeze my butt. His own feral celebrations ricocheted around the room as profanity riddled his snarls and growls.

He gently helped me up off the plug and then, with his body still connected to mine, he stalked off toward the bathroom so we could share one last sexy shower on our love boat.

CHAPTER 11

We arrived back in the true North strong and free a week after the Canadian Thanksgiving in October, blissfully happy, tanned as can be and more in love with each other than ever. But as beautiful as our honeymoon had been, we were both looking forward to rejoining reality and getting back into the routine of life.

We'd stopped off in Vancouver for a few nights to say hello to Justin and his family and then surprise Amy, Henry and James' parents by showing up to Henry's party. James had gone above and beyond like he always does, determined to show up Garret's brother and be the world's greatest uncle. He went out and bought Henry his very own child-size electric convertible car. Even though the kid was only one and wouldn't be riding it any time soon, it'd been the highlight of the party, overshadowing all other gifts, of course.

But we said our goodbyes and packed up, eager to get home and back to reality. As wonderful as our holiday had been, reality was just as sweet.

Normally early fall in Victoria is still ripe and warm, with the lingering hint of summer in the air, cooler mornings and dark nights, but overall pleasant afternoons. But when we stepped off the airplane, we were both hit in the face with a frigid smack of cold wind. It was Mother Nature laughing at us for having left the warmth of Oceania early, happy as can be, with mushy thoughts and full hearts. And like the unforgiving bitch she's been known to be, the woman decided to whack us upside the head with a big ol' dose of winter moments after hitting the tarmac.

The big, tall evergreens behind the house reminded me of those arm-flailing tube men in front of car dealerships as they tossed and jostled high and mighty in the back yard, battling it out with the first storm of the season and its ferocious gusts. And we fought those gusts with every ounce of our strength as we opened the door of our town car and heaved our suitcases from the trunk. One final wave at our driver, and the two of us were practically sprinting up the front walkway to the door.

But when we walked inside, there were lights on, and it was warm and cozy. That sneaky devil of mine, he must have called the house-keeper ahead of time and asked her to come over and light the fire-place. He grinned back at me as I looked up into his eyes, my own eyes full of wonder and love. Always the romantic, my husband, and I hoped he never changed.

Too tired to unpack, we just left our suitcases unopened in the corner of the bedroom and went about getting ready for bed. But when I came out of the bathroom after my shower, my wedding dress was lying out on the bed.

I lifted one eyebrow. "What's going on?"

James came back into the bedroom and handed me a brandy snifter with a small splash of the aromatic liquor. "I realized that you changed into shorts and T-shirt before we left for our honeymoon. I never had the chance to take your wedding dress off you. I never had the chance to fuck you wearing your dress. I want that chance."

A wry smile tugged on my lips as I took the dress off the bed and wandered back into the bathroom to go and put it on.

My dress wasn't overly complicated with a gusset or ties at the back, so I was able to slip into it without much fuss. And just to be extra authentic, I grabbed the spare garter I'd bought (in case I'd lost the other one somehow) from my hair elastic drawer in the bathroom and slipped it up over my thigh.

Giving my hair one quick finger-comb and toss, followed by two quick cheek pinches and some cherry flavored lip balm, I opened up the bathroom door and stood there. Just like it had the first time he saw me in my wedding gown, James' breath caught, and his pupils dilated.

"So beautiful," he finally managed to say, momentarily stunned and making me feel happy and girly and causing the butterflies in my belly to dance in an unmitigated frenzy.

He stalked toward me and pulled me against him, spinning me around so that my back was to his front. He started dropping soft kisses on my neck and shoulders and murmuring all kinds of wonderful things in my ear. His voice was like a zephyr against my skin, and it was driving me wild.

I turned around and looked up into his eyes. The firelight danced lambent in them. He was beautiful, masculine, and I found myself speechless and short of breath at the way his eyes were running up and down my body in awe. I still had to pinch myself from time to time that this man was my husband. He was mine, all mine, from now until forever.

My eyelids grew heavy and my pussy wet with the inebriating effects of James' skillful seduction. Whatever he wanted, whatever he demanded, I needed to give it to him like I needed air to breathe.

He nuzzled that spot where my neck met my shoulder. "The entire night is about you, my perfect wife. I plan to worship you."

Yes, please!

Scooping me up, he carried me over in front of the fire and laid me down on the white and brown llama skin, the skirt of my dress riding up and pooling around my hips. He caught sight of the garter and with a roguish smirk reached out and pulled, letting it go so it snapped painfully against my thigh. The dirty bugger. But the pain dissolved, replaced by a tender but lovely warmth as the memories of James and his diabolical elastic bands on the boat came flooding back. He pushed my thighs apart and maneuvered my legs so that my knees were bent, and then lifting my hips, he slid my underwear down past my ankles and put them to the side.

Then he went about the task of undressing himself. Sweater, shirt, jeans, socks, it was hard to believe such a mundane act, an act I'd witnessed hundreds of times over the last few years, still managed to turn me on. Still managed to rev my engine and get my juices flowing. Our eyes were fixed on each other, speaking volumes without uttering a sound. A wolfish smile crossed his lips, and the flames illuminated the already blazing passion in his eyes. He settled down on his stomach and pushed his hands up my dress, cupping my butt, pulling himself so his head was at the apex of my thighs.

"Just relax and enjoy, princess," he said, before flicking his tongue out so it grazed my clit.

So I did. For the rest of my life.

EPILOGUE

Roughly one year later...

"**I** 'm going to pee my pants," I said through gritted teeth, glaring at the woman behind the glass and willing her to tell me I was next, or that I could go pee, that a beyond-full bladder wasn't needed.

James looked at his watch. "Any minute now, babe. You're doing great. Just hold it a little longer."

I glared at him. "Easy for you to say, you ass. You didn't just chug over a liter of water. And are now going to have someone pushing on your bladder."

He went to open his mouth but was interrupted by the two most glorious words on the planet. "Emma Shaw?" said a tall and slender woman with square glasses. She was holding a chart and dressed in light-blue scrubs. "You're with me."

I scrambled to sit up, but that bit of movement just put more pressure on my bladder, and I'm pretty sure I peed a little. Fuck, fuckity, fuck!

"Just lie down on the table please, Mrs. Shaw. Pull the waist of your pants down a couple inches and your shirt up to your bra," the woman instructed.

James helped me climb up onto the gurney, and like a man who thought he was in the doghouse simply because he was the reason I was so damn uncomfortable, he removed my flip-flops for me and stowed them beside my purse.

"I've been hit by a car before." I blinked back actual tears of pain, my bladder hurt so much. "And that was nothing compared to how bloody uncomfortable and painful this is."

He pouted at me and took my hand. He knew that there wasn't anything he could say to me that would make me feel better. I'd been in a foul mood since I woke up. It was hot out, and I was exhausted. None of my clothes fit, and the only thing I could stand to put in my stomach was grilled cheese sandwiches. I'd made him throw out the peanut butter, because just the sight, let alone the smell, of his peanut butter toast in the morning made me vomit into the kitchen sink.

"I'll let you go pee in a minute, Mrs. Shaw. I won't need you to have a full bladder the entire time," the technician said, her smile the same as my husband's. Cautious but optimistic.

I let out an exasperated sigh. "Fine."

She flicked on the screen overhead and then squirted the warm gel onto my belly before placing the probe on my skin. It was almost immediate, that beautiful *thump, thump* sound. The sound that made tears sting my eyes and both James' and my face erupt into giant smiles.

"Hmm," the technician hummed, her face scrunched up in a curious scowl.

"What?" James said. "Hmm? What does that mean? Hmm?"

The woman shook her head. "Sorry, didn't mean to scare you. It's not anything bad. In fact ..." Her mouth drew up into an elated grin, as if she was getting ready to divulge the juiciest gossip to the whole neighborhood. "It's the exact opposite. This is why your doctor sent you to us a little earlier than most couples come for ultrasounds. She heard something irregular and wanted to investigate further."

"Irregular?" I asked, struggling to prop myself up on my elbows, my eyes going wild and darting around the room, to my husband, the monitor, the technician and my belly.

She shook her head again. "No, no, nothing irregular. But ..." She hit a couple of keys, and a new image appeared on the screen above our heads. "We're not hearing just one little heartbeat in there ... we're hearing two."

"Two? As in mine and the baby's?"

"No." She clicked the mouse a couple of times, and little colored dots appeared on the image. Then she labeled two of the dots, *Head 1* and *Head 2*. "Two heartbeats, because there are two babies. You're having twins, Mr. and Mrs. Shaw. Congratulations!"

James' hand squeezed mine while fresh tears pricked my eyes. Two babies! Twins!

"Twins?" he choked.

She nodded. "Yes, sir."

"Can you tell the sex yet?" James asked, his eyes glued to the screen while the technician continued to click and label. *Arm, leg, foot, eye, mouth, ear...*

"It's still a little early, Mr. Shaw. We'll have you come back in a couple weeks when the babies are bigger. But..." she zoomed in on the screen for a second and clicked a few more times.

Our eyes flew to her face.

"But what?" James asked, trying hard to be pleasant and patient, but I could tell it was taking every ounce of his self-control not to shove the woman out of the way so he could figure out the contraption himself and get down to business. He was all about efficiency, my husband. Efficiency and control, and in this particular situation, he wasn't experiencing either.

She shook her head and smiled. "But if you want to take a guess as to what *those* body parts are, right here and here ... that's the sex. But we'll wait a few weeks to confirm."

His eyes bugged out of his head. He wanted to grab her by the shoulders and shake the answers out of her.

"So, what are they?" I asked.

"I'm not allowed to say," she said with a rueful smile.

James' mouth dropped open. "What? Why not?"

"I'm just not. You'll have to wait to hear the report from your doctor. But again, it's probably best if we wait a few more weeks."

"But you *do* know what they are? You can tell right now, can't you?" The poor woman, my husband was giving her the third degree, and she was just trying to do her job.

He let go of my hand and stood beneath the screen, scrutinizing it like it was a piece of priceless art or one of the plans for a new development his company was building.

"Well, I took the test online, just in case," he started. "It was a set of thirty ultrasound images, and you had to correctly identify each image, and I scored one hundred percent." He turned back to face me. "Don't worry, Em, I got this." Then he looked to the technician again. "Can you zoom back in on their junk, please?"

Her lip twitched in amusement. "Sure. Zooming in on your babies' *junk*."

James took a step closer. Then he grabbed the spare chair and stood up on it so he was practically face to face with the ultrasound image of our children up on the big TV screen.

"Boys!" he finally announced. "Two boys. See ..." He pointed at two arbitrary spots on the screen. "There are their wangs. And what wangs! Wow, boys, good job! I'd say they take after their old man already."

He stepped down off the chair with a big grin.

"You need to go use the washroom now, Mrs. Shaw," the technician said, using a towel to wipe the goop off my stomach. "It would appear one of the babies is stuck between your full bladder and the wall of your uterus. Its head is trapped, and you need to go to the washroom and free it. That way we can continue to take some measurements."

I went to sit up, and I'm pretty sure that made me pee myself a little again. "My baby is trapped?"

She rolled her eyes. "Go free your child."

When I came back into the room, I felt a million times better. I no longer wanted to murder the man who had knocked me up and made me have to fill my bladder to the point of near bursting. I was ready to lie back down and enjoy the experience of watching the babies in my belly squirm and wriggle.

"They're definitely boys," James said again, helping me back up onto the gurney.

I looked to the technician for confirmation, but she remained indifferent. Not even the jiggle of an eyebrow.

"You don't know that for sure, James." I hiked my shirt back up, and she squirted more gel onto my belly. "I bet they're both girls and you have no idea what you're talking about."

She started maneuvering the probe around again, and within a couple of seconds, the echoing sound of *two* competing heartbeats filled the room. It was music to my ears.

"Come on," James said. I could tell by his tone that he was getting ready to lay on the charm. My current state was proof that his charm, charisma and smile could get a woman to pretty much do anything. The man's voice alone was like melted chocolate. "Come on," he said again. "No one has to know that you told us the sex of the babies. We won't say a word. In fact, we'll say that you refused to tell us." He leaned over and fished his wallet out from his back pocket. "What's it going to cost for the goods, lady?"

I snorted. The technician snorted too.

"Don't bribe the poor woman!" But then I looked at her square in the eyes. "No, seriously, how much is it going to cost?"

Her mouth drew up into a giant smile, the type of smile that one makes when they're about to do something naughty, consequences be damned. "I'll tell you this. One of you is right, and one of you is wrong." And then she went about labeling more body parts, leaving James and I staring at each other in wonder.

And this concludes *Hot and Filthy*
I hope you enjoyed this extra steamy tale

Want to know more about Justin, Kendra, James and Emma?

Stay tuned for Book 5 in The Dark and Damaged Hearts Series
True, Deep and Forever: Part 1
Garret and Amy

IF YOU ENJOYED THIS BOOK

If you've enjoyed this book, please consider leaving a review. It really does make a difference.

Thank you again.
Xoxo
Whitley Cox

SNEAK PEAK - TRUE, DEEP AND FOREVER, PART 1

True, Deep and Forever: Part 1, Book 5 of The Dark and Damaged Hearts.

True, Deep and Forever: Part 1

TRUE, DEEP AND FOREVER: PART 1 - CHAPTER 1

AMY

D ream or reality? Sometimes when you're that deep in sleep, you can't always tell. Though my delightful reverie involving Ryan Reynolds and myself sharing a bar of chocolate in the backseat of a taxi whilst driving though the mountains sure as heck *seemed* real. Until the shrill sound of a wailing baby infiltrated the wonderful moment and caused Ryan to disappear, taking my chocolate with him.

The clock said four forty-five in the morning. Jesus, child, would it kill you to sleep in now and then? God, I missed the newborn days when they slept for like twenty hours a day. I sat up and looked at the mound of man sleeping next to me. His bald head with its five o'clock shadow peeked out from beneath the duvet; a light rumbling snore vibrated in his throat. His mouth was half-cocked open, with the bum-chin trembling ever so slightly on each inhale.

Must be nice to be such a sound sleeper. The whole damn Vienna Boys Choir could be playing with cymbals in here, and Garret would sleep through the entire thing.

"Don't worry," I said, louder than necessary. "I'll get up. It's not like *I* have to be at work this morning."

"Hmmmm," he moaned, rolling over and offering me a view of his nice muscular back, causing a pang of guilt to soar through me at my initial thought. He'd worked really late last night so that he could take Friday off, crawling into bed ever so quietly after the rest of the house had gone to sleep. All so that we could go over to Victoria this weekend for my brother's wedding. I shouldn't really begrudge him a few hours of sleep.

And yet I did.

"Mumma, mumma, mumma, mumma ... " And then, "Wahh-hhhhhhh."

"I'm coming," I whispered, throwing back the covers, then snatching the robe that was lying haphazardly across the foot of the bed. "I'm coming, baby." I opened the door to Henry's room, and red-rimmed, green eyes stared up at me as he stood in his crib gripping the bars like a convict. His mop of curly brown hair stuck up in every direction.

"Mumma, mumma," he said, trying to climb the bars but failing. His blue and yellow rhinoceros sleep sack impeded his efforts.

"All right, all right, angel-pie. Are you hungry?" I cooed, scooping him up and carrying him to the glider in the corner of the room. I popped out a boob with my free hand while he perched on my left hip.

"Mummmmma!" he cried, pulling at my tank top, frantically trying to get at the goods.

"Hold your horses, you little junkie. I'm going as fast I can. You're not going to starve."

As I cradled him in my lap, his mouth deftly found my nipple, and he began frantically sucking, while his hands came up and he held on to my breast as if it were a bottle, eyes fluttering shut with a contented sigh.

The first thing people usually said when they saw Henry was what beautiful eyes he had and how striking the contrast was with his darker skin and afro-esque hair. A "real chick-magnet" or "heartbreaker," and I was sure they'd be right. My son was absolutely gorgeous. What with his father's darker-colored skin and leafy green eyes, he was a looker, all right.

But all I saw was my sweet baby, cherubic and pudgy and perfect in every way, and I wanted him to stay that way for as long as he possibly could. I allowed my eyes to close as he continued to nurse, the whole experience calming and enjoyable.

"You want me to take over?" came a groggy voice from the door. Garret stood tall in the doorway, clad only in his plaid Fruit of the Loom boxers, knuckling the sleep out of his eyes just like his son did when he was tired. He was a handsome specimen of a man, my husband, with cyclist's legs, toned arms and bright green eyes that seemed to shine in the glow from Henry's ocean-themed night light, to match his ocean-themed room. His stomach was not as taut and chiseled as it'd once been—he'd put on what he liked to refer to as "sympathy weight" while I was pregnant, indulging in my ice cream sandwich cravings right along with me. But even with a bit of a dad belly, he was still damn fine.

"You lactate now, do you?" I asked, a small smile curving up at the corner of my mouth. Henry's eyelashes trembled against his pink cheek at the sound of his father's voice, but they didn't open. He was off in a milky dream.

Garret rolled his eyes. "You know what I mean. I can put him back down when you're done if you'd like to go grab some more sleep. Or I can take him downstairs if he's up."

"I think he'll probably go back down for another hour or so," I said. "But thank you. You go back to bed. You look like hell."

"Thanks." He yawned, stretching up and grabbing hold of the doorjamb before turning around and heading back to bed.

A few minutes later Henry popped himself off and snuggled into my chest, his little mouth making the perfect *O* shape while a tiny stream of milk ran down from the corner of his lips. After laying him down in his crib and making sure he wasn't going to just pop right back up, I headed back to my own room, determined to catch even thirty more minutes of shuteye before I was forced to start the day.

Pulling the covers up to my chin, I closed my eyes. I was just drifting off when a warm arm snaked around my torso and pulled me across the bed until my body lay shrouded by a dominating frame. I wrapped my arm over his and melted into him, welcoming the warmth and comfort

of his big body. And once again sleep was just about to claim me, beck-
oning me into its delicious embrace, when I felt the all too familiar
poke of arousal on my butt and a curious hand wandered over my body
and beneath my pajamas.

I moaned. "Really?"

"It's been ages. Come on." He growled, leaning over and biting my
earlobe, a gesture that generally revved my engines but was doing
nothing for me at the moment.

"Fine," I mumbled. "Just try not to wake me in the process."

"That's no fun," he purred, shimmying out of his boxers and diving
beneath the covers, flipping me onto my back. "Come on, Ames, out of
those jammies, I want to see if I can beat my record."

I rolled my eyes. "Fine."

I had to admit it, my husband was an incredibly skilled lover, and
his tongue work was unsurpassed. Before Henry joined the team,
Garret was able to get me screaming his name and bucking wildly into
his face in under a minute, all with the flick and roll of his tongue and
some well-placed fingers.

But ever since Henry, things had been different. Sex wasn't easy, and
it wasn't as enjoyable, at least not for me. The birth hadn't been easy,
and now ... *things* were not so easy.

So, even though I was all healed up now, and the doc had given the
go-ahead many months ago that it was okay to get jiggy with my hubby,
I certainly wasn't enjoying things the way I used to. No one told me that
after you have a baby, you have to re-learn how to have sex. That you're
essentially a teenager in high school again, figuring out how to orgasm
and fumbling around with your lover quietly in the dark, choosing ten
minutes of "pleasure" over ten minutes of sleep.

Only this time you're trying not to wake the baby instead of your
parents or the neighbors in the unit next door. You and your man pant
and kiss and bump uglies under the covers, because God forbid he
actually sees your body, all jiggly and lumpy in its depressive post-
partum state. Meanwhile, milk squirts him in the eye as he kneads your
engorged breasts.

Oh yeah, so hot!

And don't even get me started on lubrication! Normally Garret would just have to look at me the right way and I'd be a slick mess in my pants. Now I was as dry as a fucking desert. Just call me Sahara or Gobi or ... those were the only deserts I could think of right now, but you know what I mean.

What used to be fun foreplay was now like heading into the salt mines. If he wanted to get me off, it was hard work and hours of repetition.

But I let him try, and try he did. His diligent tongue worked my clit until it was achy and needy. Tiny circles and long lavish licks up my cleft left me a squirming, panting mess. I was seconds from reaching my destination when a screech over the baby monitor jolted me to attention and out of my loopy, lusty dreamland.

"Waahhhhhh, mum, mum, mum, mum ... " I could practically hear the tears streaming down his little cheeks. I was pretty sure he was teething again. I tossed back the covers and motioned to get out of the bed, only instead Garret pulled my legs down and covered my body, impaling me in one solid thrust.

"What the fuck, Garret?" I yelled, swatting him on the back. "Get off of me. I need to go."

"He's fine, come on. You were so close. We can get you there again," he said with a masculine growl, bending his head low and nipping my ear.

"I'm not going to get off," I said matter-of-factly, lying there like a limp noodle as my husband pounded into me, the muscles on his arms bunching from having to carry all his weight. "And you need to put a condom on. I don't want to get pregnant."

"Come on," he said again with a grunt, picking up the pace and continuing to hammer into me. He wedged his hand between us and began rubbing circles around my clit. I wasn't going to lie, it felt good, and for a moment I was tempted to shut my ears off, wrap my legs around his waist and meet him thrust for thrust. But I couldn't. The screaming was too loud, and the way my body reacted to my crying child killed any other feelings inside me. Even desire for my husband.

"We can't," I said with remorse. "Condom or pull out."

"It's not going to happen. I'll be quick."

"Henry happened on the first try. We're fertile. Either pull out and finish yourself off or put a condom on and get the job done." I knew my husband needed the release, and even though I wasn't going to find mine, I was willing to let him find his. "Just make it snappy," I sighed, the shrieking on the baby monitor picking up vigor.

He let out his own big sigh. "Never mind, just go deal with our child." And with that, he pulled out and headed to the bathroom, muttering, "Kids are fucking cock-blockers."

***

I loved my kitchen. I loved my entire house. Seeing as we'd built it from the ground up, I'd been awarded the privilege of picking out everything from cupboards to floorboards. The morning sun burst in through the window behind the sink and caught the green jewel-toned backsplash, making it glow. I loved jewel tones and had decorated our home (tastefully of course) with the rich hues of green, amber and burgundy with the odd splash of brown and plum. I wiped crumbs off the gold-veined white granite counter before turning to face my husband. He was still in his flannel robe nibbling on an English muffin with raspberry jam and mindlessly reading the newspaper. His carbon-copy was perched in his highchair with said jam smeared across his cheek and a mushed and mangled English muffin with bite marks squished tightly in his little fist. The other fist pounded on the tray like a slave ship drum.

"Could you get him to stop that, please?" I asked, perhaps a bit too snippy as I packed all of our lunches.

Garret grabbed his son's fist and gave him a stern look while gently saying "no." Henry seemed oblivious to the discipline but found interest in his sippy cup and started gnawing on the nipple of it.

"We should see if your parents will take Henry one night for a sleepover so that we can have some grown-up time. What do you think?" Garret asked later, switching gears, seeming to have ignored my bitchy snap.

I had planned to take a full year's maternity leave and was thoroughly enjoying my time with my son, but the gallery I worked for had lost two employees in the span of a week, and another one had taken medical leave. I'd been asked to return to work three days a week with a serious increase in my pay, enough so that it was worth giving up the employment insurance I was getting paid each month. So I returned to work part-time when Henry was eight months old. Yet, despite the fact that I'd been back at work for nearly two months, it was still a huge change for our little family, especially for me as I attempted to balance work, a social life, motherhood, and being a wife.

Everyone demanded something of me. Always.

Some days it felt as though I couldn't catch a break and was failing in at least one facet of life, whether it be friend, mother, wife or employee. Other days it seemed as if I was failing at all of them and disappointing the world. It helped in the transition back to work, though, that Garret's parents had offered to take Henry. So while I was at work, I had the peace of mind knowing my child was being well taken care of by people who loved him nearly as much as we did.

Three days a week, I packed snacks and a couple of bottles of pumped breast milk for Henry and dropped him off with his grandparents on my way to work. Then his father picked him up on his way home around five-thirty. Our system had been working like a well-oiled machine for several weeks, but lately Garret had been texting me midday, asking me to pick Henry up because of an unexpected work "thing," and he was arriving home after his son had gone to bed. Last night had been one of those nights.

"So what do you think?" Garret asked again. I'd drifted off into my thoughts and hadn't bothered to answer him. *Shit.* He really was the most patient human being on the planet.

"About what?" I wrapped up his sandwich and put it in his lunch bag, along with a bag of chopped veggies and an apple. The same things made their way into my lunch bag as well.

"Getting your parents to watch the little man for a night."

"Uh, yeah ... maybe. It's going to be pretty hectic, what with the wedding and all. Might not be doable." My brother was getting married on Saturday, so there would be absolutely NO opportunity for us to get out for *drinks* with him and Emma. And my mother was spazzing out, much as she had over our wedding, and would be in no frame of mind to babysit. But I'd already denied my husband an orgasm this morning and snapped at him at least once, so instead I just nodded and hummed another "maybe."

Garret came up behind me and wrapped his arms around my waist while bending his knees, our height difference making it a tad awkward. We began to sway.

"I miss the crazy sex we used to have. I miss having sex, period. God, when was the last time we did it?"

I honestly couldn't remember.

"I miss the naughty pictures you used to text me in the middle of the day. Send me a picture of your boobs this afternoon, would ya?"

I smirked. "We'll see. I'm really busy this afternoon. We have a new artist coming in. He wants to do a show, so I've got a lot to do."

He spun me around so that we were facing each other. "Okay. Remember, you show me yours and I'll show you mine." His eyebrows playfully bobbed up and down like two dark caterpillars on his forehead before he swooped in and pecked me hard on the lips. "All right, you've got the little man? I'm going to go shower."

I nodded before turning my back to him and *then* rolling my eyes as I finished packing our lunch. I had no problem seeing his, but like hell was I going to take a selfie of *mine* and have that floating around the internet. No freaking way.

SNEAK PEEK - QUICK & DIRTY, BOOK 1

And just to be kind (and get you hooked). Here's an excerpt from Chapter 1 from *Quick & Dirty, Book 1 A Quick Series Novel,* coming March 29th, 2018

QUICK & DIRTY - CHAPTER 1

"Hey, it's me again. Look, I know you're pissed, but it's really for the best. You weren't making me happy. I need a woman who has more spark. More fire. More passion. You're like a dead fish, really. I think you might have some daddy issues there, *darling*. Not enough hugs growing up or something." His syrupy-sweet voice made me wish there was an app where you could reach inside your phone and throat-punch the caller on the other end.

How I wanted to just watch him choke and gasp for air, his smarmy eyes bugging out as his hands found their way to his neck and he looked at me in panic.

Motherfucker! Daddy issues?

Fuck him. He knows nothing about me. NOTHING!

But like the mouse that keeps going back to the same freaking trap, I put my ear back to the receiver.

"I need someone who is going to be there for me when I need her, you know? Besides, were you even happy? Half the time I can't even tell. Happy, mad, sad. For a woman who doesn't get Botox anymore, you sure have a face like one. Anyway, I just wanted to let you know I've put all your things in a box and had my chauffeur drop it off at your apartment."

Swallowing the taste of bile that had suddenly formed a thick film on my tongue, I deleted the message on my phone before his voice could continue.

Fuck him!

Fuck Xavier Rollins and his millions. Fuck Xavier Rollins and his beautiful downtown penthouse apartment. Fuck Xavier Rollins and his nice cars, his family's private jet, his enormous yacht. Fuck him and fuck everything else. Fuck everyone else. Fuck everyone he knew, he worked with, fuck them all. I was done.

I'd wasted three years of my life with that asshole, three fucking years. And apparently during the last year (but who really knew? It could have been the whole damn time) he'd been screwing everything with two X chromosomes that batted heavily mascaraed eyelashes at him. His assistant, his secretary, his kid's nanny, his ex-wife apparently from time to time. You name the bitch, and chances are Xavier had slipped his pasty-ass body between her thighs. And yet the bastard had the audacity, the *audacity* to dump *me*.

"I'm not sure it's working anymore," he'd said on New Year's Eve as we ate dinner in one of Xavier's New York restaurants. The entire place had been closed down for a private party hosted by Xavier himself. The room was packed with New York's most elite socialites and celebrities, all "friends" of the eccentric millionaire and giddy as can be to be part of such a lavish event.

"You're never around. You're always off working. And you're, well . . . " He actually had the decency to grimace slightly. "You're not exactly warm or *adventurous* in bed, darling. I need a woman who's willing to, you know . . . "

I shook my head and blinked at him a few times before deciding to open my mouth. "No, I don't *know*. What is it you would like me to do?" I scanned the nearby tables, hoping nobody was eavesdropping on us, but it was a party, it was New York, it was Xavier Rollins. People were listening. They always were. Bringing my voice down a little lower and leaning closer to him, I swallowed before speaking. "Can we not discuss this here, please, Xavier?"

He took a sip of his rye and tonic while simultaneously giving a half-wave and a smile to Gigi Hammond across the room. She winked at him and bit her lip the way a woman does when she wants you to bite her "other" lips.

"No, we'll discuss it right here. I want a woman who is adventurous."

"I'm a travel journalist. I go on adventures for work. You're not making any sense."

He coughed slightly while his eyes took on an almost bored, glazed-over look. "Yes . . . but not in bed."

Suddenly my cheeks felt as if they'd gone up in flames. "Please," I said with a hiss, "let's not talk about this here."

He flicked his wrist again as if I were not more than a pesky fly buzzing around his head, a mild irritation he could just bat away. "I'm sorry, darling, but you're boring. You're boring me. I want a woman who is around more. You're like a dead fish. Cold, boring, lifeless. We're through."

I shook my head, still not entirely able to process what was happening but nonetheless feeling the harsh sting of his words.

Cold.

Boring.

Lifeless.

A dead fish.

A distant ringing sound began going off in my ears, and my chest hurt. Was I having a heart attack? A stroke?

"What kinds of things in bed are you wanting? You've never said anything. You want me to quit my job and just follow you around like some *groupie*?"

"Not a *groupie*." He got a wistful look in his eye. Xavier had always wished he could be a rock star. Live the life of a rock star. And despite the fact that he had millions of dollars and hobnobbed with the richest of the rich, partied with rock stars and movie stars, models and politicians, he *wasn't* a rock star. He was heir to The Handy Dandy Soap Company, a big household cleaning supply company that his grandfather had founded decades ago. Sure, over the years Xavier had bought up restaurants and a couple of nightclubs, made a bit of a name for himself, but no matter how much he tried to run, he couldn't escape The Handy Dandy Soap Company or his nickname, "Bubbles."

"Not a *groupie*," he said again. "Just a doting girlfriend."

"I am. When I'm home."

"Which is not enough and why this won't work any longer," he said blandly. "You're not what *I* need. You're not *who* I want." He raised a hand and signaled the waiter for another drink. "You. Me. We're through, darling. I've moved on and so should you."

My bottom lip dropped and nearly hit the table. "You're dumping me? Here? In front of everyone?" I asked. "All because I'm not adventurous enough for you, which by the way is the first I'm hearing of your discontent with our sex life."

He looked about ready to get up and leave. Bored out of his tree and wanting to find a more lively conversation companion. "That and the fact that you work too damn much."

"But you suggested I take this job. It was your idea. I like what I do." Only when I said the words out loud, they tasted foul on my tongue, because the truth was, I didn't really like my job anymore. I was tired of it. Tired of the travel, tired of never being home more than a few days a month, tired of living out of a suitcase, tired of eating at restaurants. I wanted to cook my own meals, sleep in my own bed more than two nights in a row, and have a closet full of clothes I could stare at while complaining I had nothing to wear.

But I also wanted to do something worthwhile. I'd never understand these millionaires' and billionaires' wives who did nothing all day long, simply because they didn't have to. Even if Xavier and I got married one day, I would still want to work in some way. Devote my life to charity work or fulfill my lifelong dream of writing a book. I couldn't simply spend the rest of my days playing tennis, getting my nails done and making waitstaff feel like garbage at the country club bistro. No, I needed more.

He lifted one shoulder cavalierly. "It was either now or tomorrow morning. But I would rather take Felicity home with me tonight. So now it is." And as if on cue, his little assistant, *Felicity* with her size zero waist, Double-D chest and mile-long legs, sauntered up in a barely-there black leather miniskirt and matching crop top. Jesus Christ, how old was this chick? Xavier was forty-seven; was he old enough to be her father? I wouldn't doubt it.

Felicity perched on his knee and wrapped one svelte arm around his back, her coal-black eyes fixing me with a lethal stare.

What the fuck?

We used to be friends . . . sort of. She and I had grabbed lunch in the past. I babysat her cat, and it'd barfed all over my Aubusson rug. And now, all of a sudden, she's his new fuck buddy and I'm chopped liver?

"So . . . what? You want me to stay the rest of the night at the party, or should I just go?"

I didn't know what to do. People would be wondering why I'd left. It'd be all over social media by morning, if not sooner. The breakup, the speculation as to why. Rumors, some true and some not, flying out from every moron with opposable thumbs and a cellphone, trying to somehow cash in and weigh in on a very public breakup. And then the memes would start. I'm sure people were snapping pictures of us at this very moment. My mouth hanging open like a codfish, Xavier sitting there all smug with his hand up Felicity's skirt, her siren-red lips nibbling on his ear as if it were some piece of decadent chocolate and not old-man ear with hair sticking out of it. Well, now I wanted to barf as well as scream and throw things.

Fucking Xavier Rollins. Fucking *Bubbles!*

"Oh, no. Of course not. That would be incredibly awkward for me . . . and for you. You can go."

I gawked at him. He was dismissing me? Three years I'd wasted with this asshole, three goddamned years, and I meant that little to him that he was breaking up with me in a room full of people with his mistress perched on his lap like a puppet in a crop top. I continued to just stare at him, stare at what I was *losing.*

And then it hit me.

How had I not noticed any of this sooner? The greasy, poufy hair, the semi-squinty brown eyes, the nervous twitch in his left eye— I'd been blind to it all. Blinded by love. Because even though I'm not sure I'd ever said it to him, I did love Xavier. At least I thought I did.

"Did you hear him, Parker?" Felicity asked with an almost giggle, well, more like a cackle. "He said you can *go*."

And you can go straight to hell, you traitorous little bitch!

But I didn't say anything. Over the years I'd learned that it wasn't always important to have the last word. Sometimes the best thing to do was gather up what remained of your dignity and leave with your head held high.

I reached for my purse and my coat, then, with nearly a hundred pairs of eyes on me, I walked out of the "XR" restaurant, hailed a cab and didn't look back. And now, two weeks later, I was on the tropical island of Moorea and about to interview a billionaire.

"Stupid fucking Xavier . . . " I muttered after I thanked the man from the shuttle for retrieving my suitcase from the back of the van. I clicked the handle up and headed to the lobby to check in. "Stupid fucking Xavier. I can be warm. I can be adventurous!"

I rolled my suitcase down the slate path toward the big open doors, the rhythmic *clickity-clack* sound of the wheels on the exposed rock drowning out the din of hotel lobby noise while the strident cry of a random tropical bird punctured the air like a car backfiring in a quiet street.

I scanned the entrance into the hotel, not quite sure what exactly I was looking for but knowing I'd know when I saw it.

"Stupid fucking Xavier," I said again. Maybe I'd just sleep with the first man who said "Hello" to me. How's that for adventurous? Rock his world, give him all the warmth and attention Xavier said I never gave him. I'd give it to a complete stranger. Yeah, I'd have sex with a complete stranger. Quick and dirty sex to get over my breakup. An innocuous tropical fling. Nobody knew me here. Yes, I was here for work, but no one besides me and the owner of the hotel knew that. And as long as he didn't find out what I was up to, I could have a different man in my bed every night if I wanted. I was here for ten days; that's ten different men. This place could be my rebound playground.

The further I got into the lobby, the more I liked my idea. I was going to fuck away my worries. Fuck away my problems. Use someone else to exorcise the plague that was Xavier Rollins from my mind, my body and my soul. Now I just had to find the right guy ...

"Hello, and welcome to The Windward Hibiscus Hotel. Is there anything I can help you with?"

Eyes as green as the surrounding mountains flared with curiosity and perhaps a dollop of fear. But I hardly took notice of his eyes and their long camel lashes, because the rest of him was just that handsome ... no, handsome wasn't the right word ... yummy? Delicious? Sex on a stick? No, he wasn't a stick. Too much muscle to be a *stick*. A sex god? Yeah ... this guy was a walking, talking, sex god. He just had to be. Tall and dreamy with just a hint of danger. Muscles, toned and hard, threatened to rip right out of his crisp white dress shirt, while stubble, thick and impeccably groomed, covered his jaw, cheeks and upper lip.

Oh mama! You, you are exactly *what I'm looking for.*

Without even thinking, I gave him my best assertive stare. "Yes!" I said with a huff, lifting my head just a tad to look him in the eye. He was a good six inches or so taller than me. "You can take me into the nearest broom closet and fuck me senseless."

ALSO BY WHITLEY COX

Love, Passion and Power: Part 1
The Dark and Damaged Hearts Series Book 1

Love, Passion and Power: Part 2
The Dark and Damaged Hearts Series Book 2

Sex, Heat and Hunger: Part 1
The Dark and Damaged Hearts Book 3

Sex, Heat and Hunger: Part 2
The Dark and Damaged Hearts Book 4

Hot and Filthy
The Dark and Damaged Hearts Book 4.5

True, Deep and Forever: Part 1
The Dark and Damaged Hearts Series: Book 5

Snowed In and Set Up
Featured in the *Season of Seduction* Boxed Set

Upcoming in 2018

True, Deep and Forever: Part 2
The Dark and Damaged Hearts Series: Book 6

Lust Abroad

Quick & Dirty

Book 1 of the Quick Series

Quick & Easy

Book 2 of the Quick Series

Hot Dad

Hard Hart

Book 1 of The Hart-y Boys

Hard, Fast and Madly: Part 1

The Dark and Damaged Hearts Series: Book 7

ACKNOWLEDGMENTS

There are so many people to thank who have helped me on this daunting journey to becoming a published writer. My editor, Chris Kridler, you are a wonderful human being and I can't thank you enough for all of your hard work and help. A gem, a friend, a saviour, you are all of those and more. Thank you.

Tara at Fantasia Frog Designs, your covers are fantastic, and you are a peach. Keep 'em coming, lady!

The ladies in Vancouver Island Romance Authors, your support and insight have been incredibly helpful, and I'm so honored to be apart of a group of such talented writers.

Justine and Krista, my trusty beta-readers, I appreciate your feedback so much. You are true friends.

My super-fantastic ARC team and the members of my Curiously Kinky Reviewers group, I love your enthusiasm, your loyalty and help. These books are for you.

And lastly, the husband. Thank you for being so encouraging, supportive and understanding. For suggesting I go and sit and write in Starbucks for countless hours on a Saturday while you play tea party and have daddy-daughter dates with the Small Human. You are my inspiration for happily ever after, my everything and I love you.

DON'T FORGET TO SUBSCRIBE TO MY NEWSLETTER

Be the first to hear about pre-orders, new releases, giveaways, 99cent deals, and freebies!

Click here to Subscribe
http://eepurl.com/ckh5yT

YOU CAN ALSO FIND ME HERE

Website: WhitleyCox.com
Twitter: @WhitleyCoxBooks
Instagram: @CoxWhitley
Facebook Page: https://www.facebook.com/CoxWhitley/
Blog: https://whitleycox.blogspot.ca/
Multi-Author Blog:
https://romancewritersbehavingbadly.blogspot.com
Exclusive Facebook Reader Group:
https://www.facebook.com/groups/234716323653592/
Booksprout: https://booksprout.co/author/994/whitley-cox
Bookbub: https://www.bookbub.com/authors/whitley-cox

ABOUT THE AUTHOR

A Canadian West Coast baby born and raised, Whitley is married to her high school sweetheart, and together they have a spirited toddler and a fluffy dog. She spends her days making food that gets thrown on the floor, vacuuming Cheerios out from under the couch and making sure that the dog food doesn't end up in the air conditioner. But when nap time comes, and it's not quite wine o'clock, Whitley sits down, avoids the pile of laundry on the couch, and writes.

A lover of all things decadent; wine, cheese, chocolate and spicy erotic romance, Whitley brings the humorous side of sex, the ridiculous side of relationships and the suspense of everyday life into her stories. With mommy wars, body issues, threesomes, bondage and role playing, these books have everything we need to satisfy the curious kink in all of us.

Made in United States
Orlando, FL
03 September 2024

51050896R00100